F4 F10 Love Story of a Banker

Every Love Story has an Expiry Date

ANSHUL SHUKLA

INDIA · SINGAPORE · MALAYSIA

ISBN 979-8-89363-626-0

"Sometimes the most profound experiences come from the spaces between what is and what could have been."

Dedicated to

The loving memory of the girl I once loved yet could not marry.

Tere Jaane ka asar kuch Yun hua hai mujh par,
Teri Talaash me maine khud ko paa liya.

– Anonymous

… Otherwise, I wouldn't have found the author in me.

Contents

Chapter I.	SBTC Jabalpur	9
Chapter II.	Started with a Friend Request	27
Chapter III.	RBO Allotment	56
Chapter IV.	Embracing Office Life	77
Chapter V.	Doubt and Dilemma	131
Chapter VI.	Fresh Horizon	140
Chapter VII.	Echoes of Empathy	168
Chapter VIII.	My First Transfer	217
Chapter IX.	The Ebb of Love	246
Chapter X.	The Farewell	256
Chapter XI.	Ishita	274
Chapter XII.	Old Flames	281

Chapter 1

SBTC Jabalpur

"Mayank Sharma" I heard my name and a sense of current ran through my body. It was 16th December 2012 and I was at SBTC (Swift Bank Training centre) Jabalpur for joining as an SWO in India's topmost bank Swift Bank of Bharat. I was wearing formal pants and a plain white shirt. During those days it was once in a while thing for me to wear formals and therefore I was not very comfortable in such attire. Mr. Kashinath Daya was the Chief Manager, whom I had to report for joining formalities. He asked my whereabouts and handed me a letter and asked to be present at the 3rd floor, where all joining formalities will be done.

"Hey I am Mayank! Mayank Sharma from Katni. And u?" I said extending my hand to someone who I guessed had also arrived for joining the Bank.

I am Ankush Mishra." He replied.

Now, Ankush was my very first colleague or bank friend who I found very comfortable to talk to. He was around 5"6 tall, round face, fair complexion and was neatly dressed.

"We are called at 1 PM. Have you brought all documents?"

He asked.

"Yup! Hope they don't send me back for any stupid reason." I replied.

"Let's go out, there's still some time. I know a nice juice corner nearby." Ankush invited me.

Now I have been in hostel met new guys every now and then, but none of them asked for juice. Honestly, I was surprised or rather impressed. More often than not, friendship at college starts with a smoke or booze.

"Sure! Let's go." I said.

Ankush was a local guy from Jabalpur and was an engineer. It was quite trendy for youngsters those days to get an engineering degree and join government banks.

"I hope there are girls, otherwise it is going to be the most boring 15 days of our lives." I said.

"There are dude. I saw a few of them." Said Ankush.

"Are they good? I mean "Good" u know?" I asked in curiosity.

"You better not ask!" Ankush Said with a strange face.

I was still trying to learn the meaning of all his weird expressions.

"So, you're a fresher or what Mayank?" He asked.

"Well! Kind of. Just passed my B. Com from G. S. college and joined Mahendra for Speed test, now I am here." I replied while sipping from my glass.

"I also write blogs and web articles for small earning."

Honestly, I was very excited.

"Ruk na I will pay" I said trying to stop Ankush, but all my efforts failed as he gave 50/- Rs note to the shopkeeper saying,

"Don't worry! We are going to stay here for the next 15 days. Your turn will come." Ankush said smiling.

I just smiled back.

It was 12:55 PM and we were waiting in a group to go to the upper part of the huge building of SBTC Jabalpur.

The Background

I hail from Katni District of Madhya Pradesh, born into a humble family facing financial challenges. My primary Education was done in a Punjabi School and therefore I can read and write Punjabi language. For graduation, I came to Jabalpur in year 2008 and rented a room in Sadar and took admission in G.S. College of Commerce. I gave my first competitive exam as Swift Bank clerk and to my surprise I was selected and today I was to join the biggest bank of Bharat.

Growing up, my parents made considerable sacrifices to provide for me, striving to meet my basic needs despite limited resources. Their dedication and hard work have been the cornerstone of my upbringing, instilling in me values of resilience and determination.

Despite the financial constraints, my parents prioritized my education, recognizing its potential to pave the way for a brighter future. They ensured I attended school regularly, understanding the importance of learning in breaking the cycle of poverty.

Deeply grateful for my parents' sacrifices, I was determined to make the most of the opportunities afforded to me. I understood the value of their efforts and was committed to honouring their sacrifices by excelling in my studies and pursuing my ambitions.

Through perseverance and hard work, I aimed to uplift my family from their financial struggles, aspiring to create a better life for them. I carried within the lessons taught by my parents – resilience, perseverance, and gratitude – as I navigated my journey towards success.

Upon hearing the news of my selection in the Swift Bank of Bharat after successfully clearing a competitive exam, my parents were filled with joy and pride. In their conversation, they expressed their happiness and shared their heartfelt emotions.

My mother, overcome with joy, exclaimed, "I always knew you could do it, Mayank! We are so proud of you!" Her eyes brimmed with tears of happiness.

My father, beaming with pride, patted me on the back and said, "You have made us proud, beta. Your hard work and dedication have paid off. This is just the beginning of a bright future for you."

Feeling overwhelmed by my parents' love and support, I replied, "Thank you, Mom and Dad. I couldn't have done it without your sacrifices and encouragement. I promise to make the most of this opportunity and continue to make you proud."

In that moment, amidst our expressions of joy and gratitude, our family celebrated my achievement, cherishing years of hard work and sacrifice. We knew that this success marked a significant milestone in our journey towards a better life.

Love at First Sight

We were seated in a gigantic round shape conference hall. Entering this modern conference hall for the first time in my life, I couldn't help but feel astonished by its grandeur and sophistication. It was unlike anything I had ever seen before, with sleek furniture, high-tech equipment, and a spacious layout that left me in awe.

I had come to the conference hall for the joining formalities and document verification to begin my new job at the Swift Bank of Bharat. The significance of this moment was not lost on me. It marked the beginning of a new chapter in my life, filled with excitement and anticipation.

Taking a seat among the other new recruits, I couldn't shake off the feeling of gratitude towards my parents and the opportunities that lay ahead. Despite coming from a humble background in Katni district of Madhya Pradesh, I was now part of a prestigious institution, ready to embark on a fulfilling career path.

The atmosphere in the conference hall was buzzing with energy as fellow recruits exchanged greetings and shared their own stories of triumph and achievement. I found myself surrounded by individuals from diverse backgrounds, each with their own journey to success.

I said to myself "Welcome to the SBB Mayank."

Now, I had learnt from Ankush whose parents were also in SBB that today all documentation formalities will be completed then from tomorrow we will go through training for 2 weeks and at last we will be posted at the respective branches. As Ankush's father was also in SBB, he was far more confident than others and some of the faculties knew him. While for others like me, all of this was so fancy and new, we carried with ourselves the shyness, nervousness and a mixed sense of excitement of joining our first job.

"We are 28; a couple of guys are still missing. Listen up all you are not in college anymore. Make punctuality a habit from now on and keep an eye on watch".

Mr. R Khare, one of the faculties who were going to verify our documents, said in a strict tone. I found him scary since he kept thick beard and wore a heavy long coat.

"May I come in sir?" said two pretty eyes.

Wait a minute, it's not eyes which make sound, but mouth does. Everyone in the hall looked at the loveliest lady who had just arrived.

"Yes please!"

"And you are mis?" asked Daya sir.

"Rasika Agrawal sir" She replied and turned to take her seat. This was the first time I got to see her properly.

"Wow! "Sexy hai yar." Said Ankush who I thought was a nice guy until now. Huh!

"Bhabhi hai teri" I said with an evil smile.

Her sparkling eyes were far shinier than the sunshine itself and her features were just breath taking. She carried a nice body shape and her energy was very positive.

So, we proceeded with the documentation process and soon it was my turn.

"Mayank Sharma" I heard my name. I don't know why but I find myself in a frozen state whenever I hear my full name. Ankush pinched me and I finally stood up with my file.

They were checking everything from mark sheet to cast certificate. Then there had to be two separate character certificates from two different gazetted officers. Now, I had brought one from the Principal of a government college, but it became almost impossible for me to get the other one. Finally, my uncle came in rescue and helped me in getting it from the local police station.

"Certificate from police station? Beta it's the next step where we verify about you from the police department." Said Daya sir.

Everyone started to laugh, and I wished to hide myself somewhere. Gathering my shattered confidence, I said,

"Sir I just couldn't manage from anywhere else so…"

I was quite afraid and nervous; wrongly assuming to lose the job opportunity if I messed up with the documents.

"Fine! It will work." Mr. Daya said in a convincing tone.

I finally had a sigh of relief and went back to my seat.

Since it was being done in alphabetical order, Rasika had to wait long or rather I had to wait for quite some time for her turn.

As she approached the verification desk when her name was called, I noticed that some of the guys started to look at her, their gazes lingering on her figure. I couldn't help but feel uncomfortable witnessing their behavior.

Some of the guys made comments about her appearance, remarking on her nice figure and speculating about how good she would feel. These comments made me feel even worse, as I realized they were objectifying Rasika and reducing her to just her physical appearance.

I couldn't understand why some people felt the need to make such inappropriate remarks. Rasika was here for the same reason as the rest of us – to begin her career at the bank. She deserved to be treated with respect and dignity, not subjected to lewd comments or unwanted attention.

Feeling upset by the situation, I wished I could speak up and defend Rasika, but I found myself at a loss for words, hoping that the uncomfortable moment would pass quickly.

As Rasika finished her verification and returned to her seat, I couldn't help but feel a sense of relief. I silently hoped that she hadn't noticed the comments or been affected by them.

I carefully listened to all the conversation that she had with sir and was sad to know that she was from an engineering background. I don't know why but I presumed her to be far from my reach. I mean why such a pretty lady with an engineering degree will fall for a commerce guy like me. I was not bad either; actually, none of the guys in my batch were competition to me. But there was this possibility that she might already be having someone else.

Today was the first day when I saw her; listened to her voice and here I was imagining future with her and was also going through the insecurity and jealousy as well. Isn't it amazing how guys plan and imagine everything about a girl whom they have just seen for the very first time in their life?

Finally, the session was over, and we were asked to have tea and snacks.

I kept staring at her and suddenly a guy named Mridul approached her and started talking to her. I was like "what the fish man?"

Encountering Rasika chatting with Mridul triggered a wave of insecurity and jealousy within me. It was the first time I'd seen them together, and the fact that they both hailed from Jabalpur intensified my feelings. Seeing them share that common background made me wonder if they had a special connection that I couldn't compete with.

Insecurity hits when we feel unsure or inferior compared to others. It's like a knot in the stomach, making us doubt ourselves. Jealousy, on the other hand, is that feeling of fear that someone might take away what we cherish. It's a tough mix of emotions to handle, especially when they catch us off guard.

Even though I had not interacted with Mridul yet, but I assumed him to be a bad ass. He was a big guy I mean big in

Indian standards. He was dark, strong and very talkative. So, my weakness of not being able to start a conversation was his strength. I was losing my girl at the very first day to him. Then she said bye to him and some of her friends and left.

For today the class and gathering was over. Our documentation was done, and everyone was to join the classes from tomorrow. Though I was sad that I will not see her again today but was equally happy that Mridul will also not be able to talk to her.

We were allotted rooms in the grand SBTC. I was to share my room with Ankush, and I was glad about this as he seemed to be my only friend here. After settling in our room, we went out to have a tour of SBTC. It had a huge campus with gardens, mess, hostel, gym, entertainment room and various sports fields. We saw most of the new recruits who were present during the documentation were staying in hostel.

"Abey where is Rasika? Is she not staying in SBTC?" I asked Ankush.

"Want to check the entry registers?" he suggested.

"Damn it man!" You are a genius." I shouted in joy.

Now, everyone who checked in to the SBTC had to sign the entry registers. I even hoped to get her cell number as I had written mine while checking in.

"Where are you, where are you?" I was getting restless while looking for her details in the register.

"She's not staying in here." Ankush said with no expressions on his face after going through all the entries of our batch.

"What? Why dude? All the other girls are staying na then why the hell is she not here?"

I was irritated and just couldn't come to any answer.

"Maybe she's already having a boyfriend and might be touring around with him. You don't know girls from engineering bro. They are wild you know." Ankush said.

"Wild?" "What do you mean by wild?" My anger was reaching to a point where my head started to spin. I was curious and angry.

"You know they party and party hard." Said Ankush.

"How do you know?" I asked Ankush not believing him.

"Saale I am also an engineer na." He reminded me.

I was speechless. I had studied in a commerce school and college. Those of you who have studied in a commerce class know that ratio of girls to that of boys is on the very low side. Therefore, we mostly imagine and assume things about girls. Personal interaction is often not much. We went back to the room. Even the air-conditioned room and a cozy bed couldn't help me sleep properly that night.

Breaking the Ice

"Mayank! Wake up dude! Get ready! Mayank!"

I don't know when I slept last night. It was my roommate Ankush calling me and he was damn serious when it comes to punctuality. We had to attend our very first class at 9 AM sharp. It was already 8 AM but I had all the time in the world to get ready. Yes, being a guy, it just took me

15 minutes to be done with daily rituals of brushing, getting fresh, taking a shower and dressing up.

I wore plain black pant and a white cotton shirt just to look formally dressed and decent at the same time. We went downstairs in the mess and saw all the new recruits were already having breakfast. For a guy like me who until day before yesterday was living in hostel and was eating food from hostel mess, it was sheer delight to have smell and taste of such delicious food.

Before getting selected in SBB and coming to SBTC, I was living in a boys hostel of Jabalpur while preparing for this exam. Yes, I acknowledge that hostel days are memorable, but the food offered in mess and hostels is among the most unhealthy, unhygienic and tasteless food. Yet that was the food which nourished my body and brain to clear this exam therefore I was thankful. During my stay in hostel, I even used to get dressed and attend random marriage functions with friends just to have a taste of mouthwatering dishes with friends. Well it is very common for students living away from home isn't it? What Hirani sir has shown in Three Idiots is inspired from true events.

"Uhmm what do they have?" asked Ankush

"Poha jalebi, aloo ke parathe with dahi, bread butter and tea."

I replied grabbing him to the corner where plates were kept. We started filling our plates, making sure that not even a millimetre was left unoccupied.

Though my empty stomach was asking for more, but my mouth stopped chewing as soon as I saw her entering through the gate. Wearing a blue suit with matching handbag she made me fall in her love again.

Wait a minute! Did I say again?

"There she is."

"Ja talk to her." Ankush said pushing me to where she was standing. I turned 180 degree and went back to my earlier position with half a paratha left in my plate.

"No yar."

"Mujhse nahi ho payega."

I said with no confidence at all.

Actually, she was so stunning that approaching her felt like an impossible task to me.

She took her plate and sat with her friends.

Even Mridul was there but his eyes were on Harshita this time. She was an attractive girl too but seemed too innocent to fall for Mridul. Till now Mridul had never talked to me but today he came and introduced himself.

"Hi! Mridul from Jabalpur. And u?"

"I am Mayank and he is Ankush." I replied.

"To kisko pata rhe ho be?" Mridul asked straight away like all he wanted was to get girls and more girls.

"Haven't tried anyone though I like Aradhya and he dreams of Rasika." Ankush replied making me feel humiliated since I hadn't even talked to her for once.

"Rasika wo item?" "You know yesterday I chased her scooty after class." "She comes from Madan Mahal."

"She's quite a driver dude." "Tere type ki nahi hai."

Mridul said with an evil smile.

I did not say anything and just smiled at him though my heartbeat was winning a race against jet plane. I badly wanted to punch on his face.

At last it was 9 AM and we went to auditorium 2 for our first class. Mr. Sanat Kamath, General Manager of Bhopal zone, was to address us. As expected, it became boring after a few minutes and realizing this, Mr. Kamath cut his speech short and asked us to introduce ourselves.

"Hello everyone. I am Mayank Sharma! From Katni. I have done B.com computers."

I sat down introducing myself.

I was desperately waiting for her. Soon it was her turn and she stood up and introduced herself.

"Good morning everyone! I am Rasika Agrawal from Jabalpur only and I have done my engineering from Bhopal."

I couldn't keep my eyes away from her. She was excellent when it comes to speaking. OMG! My dream girl was right in front of me, but she didn't even notice me. Did I not even exist?

She was sitting two rows ahead of me and because of the fear of getting asked too many questions, I had decided to make myself comfortable at the back row.

"With such stupid decisions I am going to lose her."

I softly said to myself, but it was loud enough that Ankush heard it.

"Kal se aage baithenge be. Chill!" He said.

We were given syllabus, a notebook, schedule of our classes, and a couple of pens to comfortably take part in the learning sessions. Till now I was cursing myself for sitting at the back row, but everything has a bright side and I found this saying correct when the attendance sheet came in my hand. Since she was sitting at the front row, it had passed through her first and I got to see her signature. A big noticeable smile came on my face.

I touched her signature and could literally feel her.

"Tu sign dekhkar hi hila." Ankush said teasing me.

It was a boring class and like everyone else, we also somehow managed to spend the time pretending to listen to everything and replying positively by a long "Yessss sirrr".

After every couple of classes, we were allowed to have tea and snacks and at 2 pm it was lunch time.

"Chicken milega kya?" I asked the guy managing the food counter.

"Sale ur Pandit na. Lekin han hona to chahiye." Ankush replied with a wink.

I knew that even he used to eat chicken and he was a Brahmin as well.

Later we came to know that there's a separate dining hall for non-veg. But now it was too late since we already had filled our plates with Kadhai paneer, boondi raita, pulaw, papad, salad and at last ice-cream. Till now I had no luck in talking to Rasika and only the tasty food was keeping me alive here.

"Food was nice." I complemented the lady who was managing the mess.

"Well thank you!" You can write the feedback over there. She replied while mentioning about the feedback register.

As soon as I picked the pen to write my review, I saw the previous comment and I could not believe my eyes, it was Rasika who wrote "Food was okay. Do provide hand wash."

I made a note to myself about her concern for hygiene since back then I was not very hygienic. We all guys are like that and that's why we are guys. Our unhygienic practices start from hostel life and we keep doing it until a girl arrives in our lives.

Next two days were pretty much the same as we were mostly engaged in various activities by the faculties. Other than completing the study material, we also had to participate in a cultural event and sports tournament during the latter part of the training program.

It was Thursday and second last class was about to end when Daya sir announced,

"Once this class is over, all you guys have to go down for opening of account in Swift Bank of Bharat."

"Do take Rs 500/- for depositing in your own account."

After the class was over, we were standing in groups inside the branch premises which was located within the campus of SBTC. There were 3 counters for opening of account and issuing passbook. While waiting for my turn I met a gentleman who was also from my hometown and was working in that branch. I asked him about our place of posting and he assured me of good posting after training.

I saw Rasika talking to Mridul again and this time it blew my head and I straight away went where they were standing.

"So, you are from Jabalpur?" I don't know how I got such courage, but I asked her.

"Yes! And u?" She replied calmly.

"Katni. Sorry! I forgot to introduce myself I am Mayank!" I was nervous.

"I know." She replied with a beautiful smile.

What did she mean that she knows? Huh! And all this time I was thinking that she didn't even notice me.

"So where do you think, they are going to place you?" She asked me.

"I just talked to a gentleman here. He is also from Katni. Hope to get posting close to my hometown."

"Tumne lagaya koi jugad?" I asked her.

"Yup a friend of mine has asked his father who is a chief manager in SBB." Let's see.

"Wow! That's cool." I replied thinking here I am begging for some random help and she knows one of the chief managers even before joining the institute.

After getting the accounts opened everyone started to leave. Since we had our accounts opened simultaneously, we were still standing together.

"Don't you stay in SBTC?" I asked hoping to get a positive reply.

"Actually, Jabalpur is my hometown. So, I prefer staying at home, but I would be staying here for at least a couple of days before cultural night. I also want to experience it here, who knows when we will be here next time." She gave a detailed answer.

"Thank you!" I couldn't stop smiling.

"What?" She asked.

"Oh nothing. I was just thinking something."

I somehow tried not to be so obvious about my feelings.

"Okay then Bubye! See you tomorrow."

She said bye to me. She's going to see me again tomorrow. What does this mean? Does she like me? Has she fallen for me too? She already knows my name. Maybe I have been so dumb not knowing all this.

I was never in my life happier than today. I went back to my room thinking about her and found Ankush who was packing his bag.

"Are you not staying here anymore?" You are such a dear friend leaving the room so that Rasika can come. So kind of you bro thank you." I said teasing him.

"I will be back tomorrow morning and will attend the class bro."

"Have to go home for some work." Arpit was also a local so staying at his own house was also an option for him.

"Ok milte hain fir bhai." I said hugging him.

Ankush left me alone that night and it allowed me to have some privacy. I opened my Samsung Y Pro and typed in browser www.literotica.com.

Chapter-11

Started with a Friend Request

Next morning, I woke up early and found my cell phone's battery low. While plugging in the charger I opened FaceBook to check new feeds.

"No friend requests." I said to myself. Well it's the same story with most of the guys.

FB makes numerous suggestions about new friends and then an idea clicked in my mind. I scrolled up and in the search bar typed "Rasika Agrawal" and clicked enter button. There were hundreds of results with that name, but it did not take me long to find her. I recognized her profile because she was using her own photo as her profile picture which was quite rare those days for most of the girls. I saw all her photos from several albums and then downloaded into my phone. It was sheer delight for me to see her different photos as she hadn't locked it through privacy hammer. Man, she made my day, but viewing her photos was not my only motive of searching her. I clicked on 'Add Friend' button and the request was sent.

"Kya kar diya be? What if she doesn't accept?" Ankush said while taking a bite of banana which was in the breakfast today.

We were having breakfast in dining hall and I told Ankush about sending friend request to Rasika on Facebook.

"Why are you always so negative be?" I said in an irritated tone. Just after finishing our breakfast, we entered the class.

Even after the first day lesson I didn't sit at the front row. Mridul was sitting beside me today and this was the first time we talked in person for a longer period.

Talking and spending time with Mridul, I realized that he was not an asshole as I thought. We became good friends and he even assured me to help in impressing Rasika. The day was quite boring, and I hardly got any chance to talk to her, though we met again while writing feedback during lunch.

"Hi!" I said in a nervous tone.

"Hey had lunch?' She replied in her usual energetic voice.

"Yup and you?" I asked her even though I knew the answer.

"Well I am writing the feedback so you can guess." She said with a wink.

I just smiled as she left.

Later in the evening:

"Mayank play slowly I can't hit the shuttle this fast."

We were in the badminton court and I was playing with Leena. We had teamed up against Ankush and Aradhya. I planned this game so that Ankush who was yet to make any progress with Aradhya gets some time with her. After some while Aradhya had a phone call so Ankush also sat down saying he was tired.

"Are you also tired Mayank?" Asked Leena.

"Nope! Let's play." I replied while changing sides.

I was wearing a balloon pant with windcheater and she was displaying her assets wearing just tees and lower. I never noticed this but today I was treated with a nice view every time she bent to pick the shuttle.

She had long I mean really long hair, big beautiful eyes and was tall. But still she wasn't as beautiful as Rasika of course. I don't know if she was doing this intentionally or it was just my imagination, but I could see way more than needed while playing badminton with her.

"I have to go get some sleep now." I said realizing that it was not going the way I wanted. I planned this for Ankush but here another story was in progress and even though unintentionally, but I was gradually becoming the Hero in that.

"Okay let's put the net and everything back to the store." Leena said in a noticeable sad tone.

Every day we had to bring sports kit into the court to play and practice different games as there will be a tournament in next week. Chess, badminton, TT were the games that we had to participate in and the top 3 winners were to be awarded on the last day.

"Goodnight Mayank." Said Leena.

"Goodnight!" I said and walked back to my room. We were playing badminton in the court which was at the ground floor and first floor was allotted to the girls while boys were at the second and third floor of the hostel. It took me a few minutes to finally reach my room.

Ankush was already asleep and it didn't take me long either as I slept in a few minutes.

Next morning it was Friday and the fifth day of our stay at SBTC and Rasika was practicing TT for her qualifier. God, she played good and I didn't even know the first or the last 'T' of TT. I made a mental note to at least learn the basics of Table Tennis so that can impress her. She was quite smooth, and her moves were good. Even someone like me who had never played this game could say that her game was good.

I stood just opposite so that can make eye contacts with her. She immediately noticed my presence and smiled, and I smiled back. God! Every time she smiled my heartbeat rose like anything. You know that feeling of completeness just like that song "Tere siva duniya me rakhha kya hai" kind of.

"So, you sent a friend request in FB?" She asked still smiling while wiping sweat from her pretty face after the game.

"Nhi bhejni chahiye thi kya? Anyways you accepted it" I said with an evil smile.

"Nhi yar! "I mean why only me? I know that no other girl in our batch has received your friend request." She questioned.

"Just like that, you know!" I replied feeling shy.

"Are you on whatsap?" She said boldly asking for my number.

"Yup!" I said holding myself some more and not sharing the number easily.

"Give me your number I will add you." She said not looking at me.

"Its 7879...... and urs?"

"Message check kar lena." Saying this she left.

Soon I received her message on whatsapp and that day we chatted in whtsap for long. It was Saturday and I was only going to see her in the next class of Monday.

"Can you come tomorrow?" I sent a watsap message.

"For what? It's Sunday and there is no class." She replied immediately.

"There are several things that need to be discussed about the cultural event." I made an excuse.

"Anyone else coming?" She asked getting a hint of my doubtful intentions.

"Yes, most of them are coming." I lied to her.

"Ok I will try." She replied.

"Only try?" I said pushing my luck further.

"Ok I will be there by 2 pm." She assured.

"Come by 1 pm atleast." I pushed further.

"Why?" She again asked curiously.

"Lunch is served till 1:30 on Sunday." I replied smartly.

"So, you are asking me to have lunch with you huh?" She was in a doubt.

"Well! Kind of." Though I was typing but I couldn't stop smiling.

"Ok done! Bye for now my battery is low." She finally confirmed her arrival.

"Bye!" I replied and literally jumped in joy.

Next day I woke up and was done with shaving and haircut till 9 AM. When it was 11 in the morning, I was all set to meet her alone for the first time. I sent her a message,

"Ready or not ma'm?"

For the next 25 minutes I did not get any reply and was getting restless, checking my phone again and again. As I was about to go out for a walk my cell phone beeped, and I saw her reply,

"About to reach. Was getting ready so couldn't reply sorry."

She surprises me every time I thought to myself. 10 minutes later I saw her entering through the gates in her Scooty Pep; 'Maal Gadi' what we used to call it then.

"Hi!" she said.

"Hi!" "Let's go and have lunch, I am starving." I said leading her to the dining hall.

We entered into the dining hall which was almost empty and nobody from our batch was present there.

"Take salad! Lots of salad as it helps improve skin tone." I said while we were filling our plates.

We sat down in a corner and to her surprise it was only two of us.

"Where is everyone else?" She asked.

"They suddenly planned to go to Bhedaghat Dhunadhar waterfall." I replied while taking a bite of the papad.

"And you? Why did not you go with them?" She was curious.

"I had better plans for today." I replied smiling and she smiled back knowing what I meant.

"So finally, it's just two of us. What are we going to discuss?" She asked.

"Yup! Now I don't think we can plan anything about cultural event." I replied pretending to be upset.

"So, you play Table Tennis?" I asked trying to change the topic of conversation.

"Wanna play?" She invited me.

I was delighted as my plan was working smoothly so I agreed,

"Sure!"

As we entered the TT Hall, Mridul was already there playing songs in FM. Actually, there was a Bluetooth speaker in the TT Hall which was given to us to practice for the cultural event and later we found that it also played FM. Therefore, Mridul and I thought to use it while I play TT with Rasika.

"Hi Mridul so you are also here?" She asked in surprise.

"Hi! Yes, Rasika as I had nothing to do today." Mridul replied smiling.

We started playing TT and she displayed her skills from the very beginning. I did not tell anyone but from the last two days I had been practicing TT with Reddy sir who was the best TT player of our batch. I was leading till the half mark, but suddenly the Baazigar dialogue came in my mind,

"Haar kar jeetne wale ko Baazigar kehte hain." And thus, I lost to her intentionally.

"Yippiee! I won." Rasika screamed in joy as she won the last set.

Though I lost, but during the game I never missed a chance to see her from different angles. I even intentionally dropped the ball far at the corner so that she had to bend and her small top and Capri never helped her covering.

Mridul was helping in setting the mood by playing romantic songs in FM throughout the time.

"I am tired and have to go now as it's already 6 PM." She said while drinking water from the glass. I just kept looking at her lips wondering how lucky the glass was.

"Okay let's go I will accompany you to the gates." Finally biding goodbye, I was happy to have spent a great day with her.

It was 9 PM and I was already in my bed alone as Ankush had to go home again. I was about to sleep when her message came "Had a wonderful time with you. Thanks! Goodnight!" It was Rasika.

I replied, "You made my day". "I can't wait to see you tomorrow". "Goodnight."

She's Really a Wild Thing

It was Monday and second and the last week of our training program had started. I woke up early that morning and after getting done with the breakfast, I sat in the huge garden in front thinking about the possibilities as far as branch posting was concerned.

I was sitting watching guys wandering here and there suddenly I saw her, no not Rasika but a girl I did not even know the name of. She was from the next batch I assumed as she carried a trolley along and was dressed in casuals. I could not remember where I had seen her, but somewhere I had, and I was damn sure about this. As I was lost in my thoughts a familiar voice came,

"Hi!" It was Shalini.

Shalini wanted to be the anchor in cultural event. She was tall, fair and overall was a good-looking young lady. Though I did not like her accent.

"Hey Hi!" "How's your preparation for the event?" I asked her.

"Nothing much yar. Can't find a partner yet." She replied pretending to be upset.

"Don't worry we still have 5 days left na, you will find someone. You can ask Avinash as he was willing to anchor the event." I tried to show sympathy.

"Hey! Why don't you take part as an anchor with us?" Shalini asked me.

"Nahi yar mera mood nhi hai." I replied coldly.

Actually, I wanted to anchor the event with Rasika but Shalini and few other girls envy her and did not want that to happen.

"Achha! Take my number and share with me if you have any ideas about the event."

"Just make sure not to share it with anyone." She said while passing her number on a paper to me.

"Don't worry! I won't." I smiled knowing what she meant.

She left for breakfast and I went to the class even though still half an hour was left for the class to start. I sat thinking about the recent developments in my life and how will it affect my future. Just after a few minutes Rasika came in,

"Hi!" she said with a beautiful smile.

"Hey, you are early today." I said in a joyful tone.

"So are you!" She said while putting her bag under the table and taking her seat beside me.

After spending more than half of the training period, this was the day when she finally sat with me in class for the first time.

Earlier I was continuously listening to the song "Kabhi to pas mere aao kabhi to nazren mujhse milao" and today I felt like finally my prayers in the form of this song have been answered.

"What does the syllabus say for today?" I asked her to start the conversation.

"It says that I haven't received any roses yet." She said without looking at me.

"What?" I was shocked.

She was still not looking at me and took out a rose from her bag. I was stunned and felt myself to be extremely dumb. Usually, guys bring roses but here she was giving it to me.

"Mere ghar me laga tha. Sunder hai na?" She asked while giving it to me.

"It's beautiful yar." I was speechless.

"Peechhe dekha hai SBTC ke garden me there are big pink roses, rare to find." She said while mentioning from the window.

"Kal subah laata hun pakka." I said gathering my self-confidence.

"Rehne do Sharma Ji tumse na ho payega." She said teasing me.

"Arey haan."

"Dekh lena." I said smiling. I was loving this conversation.

As we were having a great time flirting endlessly, Shalini entered the class,

"Hi!" She said and kept her files on the second row. As she was about to leave, she said, "Aram se han camera lage hain."

We just smiled at her. I haven't told Rasika about Shalini giving her number to me yet. Till now most of our batchmates had noticed us getting closer and they knew that something was cooking.

Finally, the class started, and we were taught how to create CIF (customer information form) which was mandatory for opening of any bank account. Though I never in my life had problems with computers or learning, but today I found it difficult to understand. Maybe it was because of sitting at the back row that I could not hear what Chaterjee sir was saying. Having Rasika seated beside me helped a lot. Her voice was also louder than me and while everyone had to get their entry cleared from Chaterjee sir, I was unable to get my number verified since my voice was not loud enough to reach to sir. Rasika shouted for me, and I was embarrassed as sir listened to her and my entry was passed.

"Wow impressive! You definitely are a smart girl huh." I praised her.

"To kya! Topper thi mai apni class me." She said accepting the compliment.

"Backbenchers, Stop talking." It was chaterjee sir knowing it was us making the noise.

We could not stop laughing after his remarks. I was thanking my fortune; how painful it was to see her talking to other guys in the class and now I am sitting with her having the best time of my life.

Once the class was over, everyone was asked to stay so that a rough outline could be drawn about the cultural event. Everyone had ideas but in girls it was obviously Rasika who stood up and from guys Rahul came up to lead and prepare. I suddenly felt extremely jealous seeing him close to her. She was very comfortable with him, and it made me feel very insecure. I had not yet proposed her and so was still afraid of losing her. Rahul was also an Engineer from Bhopal and was not bad looking at all, most importantly he had brain. The way Rasika was making eye contacts longer than normal with him made me feel angry.

So, after half an hour of thorough discussion most of the roles were assigned. It was Ankush who later informed me about it as I was upset and had left to the badminton court.

Tomorrow was Christmas and it was a holiday. It also meant that SBTC was going to remain empty as most guys were partying and girls were planning to go and tour around the city. It was 9 pm and I and Mridul were carrying Blenders Pride hiding in a backpack along with some chakna. Drinks were not allowed in SBTC, but we did not care. We had decided to have party in our room. Soon enough, drinks started playing with our nerves and everyone started talking nonsense.

I messaged her,

"So, everything decided about the cultural event?"

"Yup! But where were you during the discussion?" She asked.

"I thought I was no longer needed so I left." I replied angrily.

"Oh, common Mayank. It was just genuine discussion about the event and nothing else. Please don't be upset." She tried to explain.

I couldn't go any further in this topic since I had not yet expressed my feelings to her. So, I just replied, "Okay."

"So, what's up?" She asked.

"Having party what about you?" I replied.

"At home watching TV. How's your party like?" She was curious.

"We party hard, got blenders pride here." I replied proudly.

But immediately I started regretting. I shouldn't have said that I thought to myself as I did not know if she was the kind of girl who accepts occasional drinking.

"I personally find Signature better." She replied boldly.

"Come tomorrow we can have some." I was brave enough to invite her.

"Done, but make sure no one gets to know about this." She said.

"Leave it on me." I replied.

Now you may be the least talking guy of your group, but alcohol does boost your confidence and if used smartly, it can help you big-time in life.

Next day I woke up at 9 AM and it was 10:30 in the morning when I was finally ready. There was this wine shop nearby SBTC. I went there and brought a quarter of Signature and from a general store purchased Sprite and some snacks.

As soon as I entered my room she called, "I am here in the lobby. Where are you?"

"Just coming you stay there." I said. I was extremely excited. I called Ankush who was there with Rahul and Mridul in the other room.

"Dekhna han bhai aa rhi hai wo." And hung up.

It was quite risky that a girl in a professional training institute was coming in a guy's room, so I had asked my friends to make sure nothing goes wrong. Not only consumption of alcohol was prohibited inside SBTC, but we were also strictly warned by the faculties that guys and girls must remain in separate rooms. I invited her breaking all the rules and she also accepted this proposal. We could have lost our jobs if anybody came to know about it.

I went down to the lobby and she was there in a casual checked shirt and jeans looking smoking hot.

I took her bag and said, "Let's go up."

"Mayank kitni ladkiyon ka bag utha chuke ho aise?" she asked smiling.

"Tum pehli ho." I replied which was very much true.

"Liar." She said punching me on arms not believing me.

I opened the room and hurriedly let her enter then closed the door.

"Why are you closing the door?" She was worried.

"Trust me! Not going to do any harm to you. It's just not safe someone seeing us together having drinks." I said while filling her glass. Yes, I was very quick with the drinks since all the arrangements were already made and we did not have much time either.

"By the way I have something for you"

I was on my knees and offered her pink rose which I plucked this morning from SBTC garden.

"To the most beautiful girl that I have ever met."

"Awww!" "So, you have this romantic side too." "Thank you Mayank!"

"Don't we have lemon?" she asked with her glass in hand.

"No yar, it was not available anywhere." I replied.

Honestly, I was also new to the world of alcohol and was not aware of the different combinations that people make while drinking. It is not that lemon was not available near SBTC, but back then I was not even aware of this combination.

She started feeling dizzy after the second round of drink.

We were making regular eye contacts and I said, "You are looking gorgeous Rasika."

'Uhmm really?"

"2 pegs andar gye nhi aur gorgeous dikhne lagi?" she said while looking in my eyes.

It was the moment we could not keep our eyes off each other and then it happened. Our lips met and it was a soft and wet kiss. She was extremely passionate and soon we were lying in bed hugging each other tight. I kept kissing her and soon my hands unbuttoned her shirt. It was a treat to see her without shirt.

"Itni nhi pee hai Sharma ji." She said pushing my hands away which was trying to unfasten her bra too. She suddenly pushed me and tried to run to bathroom but fell and I helped her there. She resisted a lot, but my hands had already done the trick, she was topless.

"Beautiful!" I said. We were standing in front of mirror both topless.

She kissed me again after vomitting and got herself cleaned. She kissed my neck and marked it there.

"What the hell?" I said looking at the dark red mark on my neck.

"What did you do Rasika" I was scared and asked her while looking at the strange mark on my neck.

"Well, it seems you got the first love bite of your life honey." She said and finally left the room. Today when I look back, I realize how stupid I was or rather innocent that I did not know what a love bite means. I came out of the room after 15 minutes so that nobody will doubt that we were together. Stand collar of jacket was to hide my mark as it was easily visible on the upper neck and throughout the time, I had to adjust so that noone could get a clue about our little secret.

She was sitting in the hall where event was to be held during cultural night and some of our batchmates were practicing. I went there just watching her and she smiled naughtily. Both of us were unable to stand properly and one could guess that we were drunk. As soon as I found her alone, I went near her.

"Yar chocolate laye kya mayank?" She had asked me to bring it after vomiting.

I gave her Dairy milk Silk and her expressions were like she would have kissed me right there in front of everyone.

Finally, she was gone by 5 pm and I went back to my room extremely delighted with what had happened today.

Are You Serious?

It was early morning and I was in the gym next day. Though I wasn't very muscular but was quite fit in comparison to the guys in our batch. Aradhya and Leena were already there in the gym.

"Good morning Mayank" They said in union.

"Good morning"

"You guys are up quite early?" I asked.

"We have no one to keep us awake till late night so woke up early."

Said Leena in a teasing tone and it confirmed the fact that I and Rasika were the hot topic of discussion in our class. I just hoped that they do not know about yesterday's event.

I only smiled and started warming up. After working out for some while I went up to my room, got ready and had breakfast.

Class was fine today and Rasika sat with me the whole day and we had great time together.

"I want to talk to you about something important, meet me in the garden in 10 minutes." Rasika said this to me and left with Harshita.

I went straight to the garden thinking what she must have to discuss since we talked a lot today in the class and yet she invited me to talk about something which was to be discussed alone. Honestly those ten minutes were quite difficult for me. It is normal for human mind to think of the worst scenarios in such tensed situations.

"Is this the time to part?"

"Does she has someone else, and has called me here to inform about it?"

"Did I do something wrong?"

I just couldn't come to the answer of any of these questions.

Almost half an hour must have passed and as I was deeply lost in my thoughts, I saw her coming. Man, she really is pretty, I thought in my mind not able to hide the smile.

"Hi! Sorry I am late, I said ten minutes, but you seem to be sitting here from quite some time." She said.

"Nope. Its fine I like it here. So, what is it that you wanted to talk about in private?' I asked.

"Listen Mayank! We are getting popular in our class and even my friends are asking what it is between us. So, I just want to ask you on a serious note do you really love me or is it just a time being attraction?"

"I want an honest answer Mayank." She sounded damn serious.

"I do have very strong feelings for you Rasika." Though I said her instantly, but her question raised several thoughts in my own mind. I did not know if I was really sure but at that moment I just said, "yes".

"Are you sure na? I mean you don't need to do it just because I will be hurt." She said with tears in her eyes.

"No na babe I do love you Rasika." I said.

"Please don't cry I am here, and my feelings are genuine." I tried to convince her.

"Okay! Thank you!" She smiled.

I left to my room, and she went to her room which she shared with Harshita since from today onwards she was staying here in SBTC. Once I reached my room, I messaged her,

"Can I come to your room tonight?"

"Harshita hai na babu sath me." Her reply came immediately.

"Get rid of her na" I was restless.

"Try to understand na babe." She replied.

Then I did not message her and we only met after dinner. Everyone performing in the event was gathered at the 2nd floor for rehearsal. I was just watching her being too friendly to Rahul again and it made me go mad. In order to make her jealous, I started talking to Shalini who had an obvious soft corner for me. Though Rasika noticed me doing that but she continued with her discussion and it hurt me. It wasn't long that she came to me and while holding my hand said,

"I am all yours and you don't need to feel insecure. Don't be such a kid babu okay."

Though we were at the corner, but it was visible to everyone that she was holding my hand and even Rahul saw that. It did feel like heaven to me.

"Stop talking to Shalini." She was furious about her and it made me laugh out loud.

"Okay I won't na unless she starts the conversation." I said smiling.

She gave me a tight punch and I again laughed hard.

It was 11 PM and everyone started leaving after the discussion was over. Rasika left without even saying bye to me and I again felt strange. I just couldn't understand or justify some of her actions. As everyone left, it was only Mridul and Ankush and they dragged me back to the room. As I was entering my room, I received a message,

"No goodnight kisses for me?" It was Rasika.

"Are you mad? I mean mai yahan itne ladke tum wahan itni ladkiyan?" Poore campus me camara lage hain." I was confused.

"Stairs me nhi lage hain." She replied with a wink emoticon.

"Coming in two minutes, be there."

I messaged her and left without saying anything to Ankush. I tried my best not to make any noise and reached that part of stairs which wasn't covered by CCTV and found her standing there, waiting for me.

"Come here" "Uhmm I thought you won't even say good night to me." I said hugging her tightly.

"Not possible babe." She replied.

"Uhmm so soft you are" I said tightening my hug.

We kissed for more than a minute and it was a wet one.

"Go now" she said while pushing me.

"Goodnight baby." I had to leave even though I did not want to.

As I entered the room Ankush asked where I had been. I just said that went to meet Rasika but did not say anything about our romantic adventure.

I slept well that night as finally everything was fine between us.

The Sports Night

It was 6 AM and I was awake because Rasika was in the same building. Every morning there was arrangement for coffee in SBTC outside every two rooms. Coffee / Tea were only available till 7:30 AM, so I rushed outside. Rahul, Mridul and Ankush were already there reading newspaper.

"Good morning bhai log" I said while filling my coffee mug.

"So, Mridul any progress with Harshita?" I asked.

"Yes, bro but she's just a kid you know." He replied.

"Today it's our turn for speech na, have you prepared your part?" Rahul asked me.

"I am going to speak on Search Engine Optimization." I said.

Every one of our batch of 28 were given a topic to speak on and my topic was Search Engine Optimization (SEO). Before joining the bank, I was working as an SEO writer, so it was an easy task for me.

Till now we all had mingled very well with each other and were quite comfortable in discussing any topic.

Soon everyone was in the classroom and as usual I and Rasika sat together. Our constant conversations were always a disturbance for the class, but we never listened to what they said.

"Today is my final match." She said.

"Don't worry you are easily going to win baby."

I said knowing her TT skills.

"I am not worried about TT, but the badminton game with Shikha."

She said in a tensed tone.

"Hmm she plays well."

"I have seen her playing." I said.

In the evening, we were walking outside after dinner in the garden of SBTC.

"I want to kiss you." I said without looking at her.

"Himmat hai?" she challenged me.

"Aap andaza bhi nhi laga sakti mohtarma."

I replied in a funny tone.

"Himmat hai to abhi is jagah kar ke dikhao."

She said while challenging me with an evil smile.

Without wasting any moment, I pinned her against the wall, and we smooched. It wasn't a long one, but we did it and ran since there were cameras all around. Let me tell you guys, before meeting Rasika, I wasn't this bold. Even without cameras it was an impossible task for me to kiss a girl in an open place and I had no experience with girls in past too. I don't know how this bravery came in me that I kept doing unbelievable stuff to make our stay in SBTC a lifetime memory.

At night in the badminton game, she lost to Shikha and was very upset about that. It also meant that my goodnight kiss had to wait tonight. I managed to cheer her reminding of the huge win in Table Tennis since in TT there was no match to her.

It was late night, and we were still talking on phone.

"Mayank only 3 days are left and then we will have to separate. I am so nervous. What if they gave us branches that are too far from each other? I can't live without you na." She was almost sobbing.

"Don't worry Rasika anyhow we will manage." Though I said so but deep inside same thought was bothering me too.

"Chalo let's sleep and we will see okay, don't worry." I said.

"Okay na! Thanx mayank! Love you. I really miss you." She said.

"Love you miss you hug you kiss you!" I expressed my love in usual tone to her.

Saying so I hung up the phone. That night I could not sleep, thinking of what she had said. In next three days our lives were going to change completely.

A Festive Affair

I got up early and was ready till 8 AM and today was the cultural event. We had to perform at night, and we were yet to practice for the complete show. Finally, after breakfast Rahul approached me and said "Bhai tu anchoring kar na yar."

"Rahul bhai Avinash kar to rha hai." I said trying to escape.

"Budhapa lagega sab yar. He replied.

I started laughing. "Majak nhi kar rha mai Mayank think about it. Tere aane se it will bring some charm to the stage and whole program."

"Mere maze thode kam lo bhai." I replied smiling.

"Think about it."

Saying so Rahul went to the class leaving me in self-doubt.

Later everyone insisted me to share the stage with other anchors and I could not say no when even Rasika insisted to do it.

We had taken permission from Daya sir for extra time for practice and thus the last two classes were free for practice. Anchoring an event was not a big deal for me since I had done it in school and college before. Though not completely satisfied, but we were confident about a decent performance at night after rehearsing twice.

"Mridul mai bhi chalunga bhai Sadar tak."

I said to Mridul who was going for shopping before the event. It was a special event, so everyone wanted to look good. Initially I had planned to wear a suit but later on settled with a party wear shirt along with tie and Jeans as it would make me look smart and casual at the same time.

I had a rented room in Sadar area of Jabalpur and unlike others, I was not going to shop anything as my budget didn't allow me to do so but went there to bring some of my stuff.

I met Imran and Shahwaz bhai who were my close buddies residing just beside my room. They were extremely happy to see me almost after two weeks.

"Mayank bhai it's been several days since we last saw you. How are you? Your face is glowing what is the secret?" Both of them asked me.

"It is indeed very good brother. The stay and facilities at the hostel in SBTC are top notch and the secret to facial glow is the food. The food they offer is far better than what we eat here in the mess." I explained them in excitement about the food and stay facilities of SBTC.

"Mayank bhai koi mila kya I mean mili kya?" Imran asked in his usual funny tone.

"Lagta to hai yar Imran." I replied in his tone and we both started laughing. I informed them about anchoring the event and they wished me luck. Before returning back to SBTC, I also visited my aunt who supplied Tiffin during my stay in Jabalpur. She blessed me and was glad for my achievement. After getting all the tasks done, I took an auto and reached SBTC to get ready. It was 6:30 PM when I called Rasika and enquired what she was up to and she said,

"Han baba abhi just start kia hai ready hona, Harshita is in the bathroom right now."

I did not ask her about Harshita, but she indirectly invited me by saying her roommate was in the bathroom and she was alone in the room. I went to her room and closed the door.

"So how do I look?" I asked hugging her from behind.

She was wearing bangles when I came in. Then she turned to see me pretending to be angry and said,

"Harshita hai na bataya tha still u came huh. By the way you're looking quite dashing."

"Ye bhi to btaya tha ki bathroom me hai."

I said smiling and she blushed while shushing me.

All the while we made sure no sound was made to let Harshita know about my presence. We kissed for good 2-3 minutes before she pushed me out of her room.

Finally, it was time for the cultural event which started around 8 PM. Most of us were present at the event making sure everything from music to podium and speakers were working properly. Then she came and I must say she had saved her best looks for this night. Her face glowed like full moon while she wore very light makeup wearing a black saree. When our eyes met, she smiled, and I smiled back. Ohh dear lord she made my heart beat faster.

It started with the welcome song and then it never stopped as we rocked the night with everything going as per the plans. All the faculties were happy and proud of our presentation. I was a little sad as the journey was going to end now, and I was going to part from the most special girl that I have just met. Realizing this fact, I went out alone and kept walking for some while. My phone was ringing but I never wanted to receive knowing it was Rasika. I didn't know the reason of my strange behaviour. I sat on footpath still dressed up and people going by stared at me like I was drunk. After half an hour when I felt normal, I went back and realized that cake cutting was already done and group photos were being taken. I saw Rasika talking to Rahul and again I felt extremely jealous. Suddenly Shalini came in with cake in her hand and fed it to me forcefully and I could not resist. Then I saw Rasika and she was furious after watching Shalini feeding me. Mridul was also there and asked me,

"Where have you been dude? She has been looking for you ever since you were gone. Tere lie abhi tak khai nhi bol rhi thi she will only eat with you."

I was speechless and straightway went behind her. She was sitting alone in the garden and I apologized to her and offered Silk, her favourite chocolate, which she grabbed from me. We were back for the dinner and then she told me that Harshita was going back home tonight with other girls. I was delighted to hear this news as this would also mean that I may get a chance to spend this night with her. Everyone went to their rooms after dinner, while some of the guys went out to party. I wanted to go to her room but was looking for a pretext and there was a guard outside, so I came up with an idea. I pretended to bring a blanket, to Rasika's room. It was 12:15 AM when I called her,

"Baby aa rha hun keep the door open."

"Okay babu." She said

Keeping the noise as low as possible I went to her room. My biggest fear was the guard who kept making rounds around the premises of SBTC at night to catch something similar to what I was doing. I had a blanket with me as a safety measure so if I got caught, I will pretend to be giving it to her.

I reached in front of her room safely without being noticed and slowly pushed the door and got in. She was there standing in the same Saree which had taken my breath away a few hours ago.

"I did not say earlier but you are looking gorgeous today baby." I said while closing the door and hugging her.

She hugged me tightly "Liar." That was all that she could say.

I now noticed that she had decorated the bed with red roses and a candle was lit in the corner and all other lights of the room were off. Soft romantic music was also playing in her phone.

"Ban gaye ho tum mere khuda"

I still remember the song she was playing. Ever since the beginning, fragrance and music has this effect on me that it takes me back to old days. Even today when I listen to this song, those memories start playing as a video in my mind.

That night we slept together for the first time, but it was not lust but pure feeling of love and respect. We hugged each other tightly under the same blanket and slept.

It was the best night of my life and remembering and writing about it now making me shiver. Finally, it was 4:30 AM and my phone started ringing. It was the alarm which I had set as this was the safest period to go back without being caught. One last time we hugged, though she did not want me to leave but I had to, and she also understood. Then I silently left to my room and saw that the guard was also sleeping on a chair.

Chapter III

RBO Allotment

"Today is the last day of your stay and training at SBTC."

"RBO allotment letters will be given to you during post lunch session."

Daya sir informed us about the importance of today before commencement of class.

Everyone was nervous about the allotment of RBO since we all wanted to be placed at our hometown. Unlike other jobs, in a Public Sector Bank, one is not aware of the actual place where he/she is going to work until one joins the branch. RBO is the Regional Business Office where we have to report and then each RBO is having more than 50 branches, one of which we will be posted at and order for the branch will be issued from RBO as per its requirement.

But more than the nervousness, there was this feeling of extreme sadness because of the realisation that we were going to leave SBTC today. It was not just Rasika but overall stay at SBTC that I and we all were going to miss for the rest of our lives. It had created deep memories in our hearts.

The time we had spent specially I and Rasika, those memories were making us cry and it was visible from our faces.

Yes, we did not want to leave SBTC. If possible, we would have spent all our lives in SBTC only.

"Ankush bro make some Jugad for me also na."

I requested Ankush who I knew already had asked his dad to place him at the best possible branch in Jabalpur.

"Bhai karta hun bat, but as far as I know, nobody is going to be placed in Jabalpur centre. It is already having excess staff."

Replied Ankush.

"And it means? What options are we left with?" I asked nervously.

Knowing it will not be Jabalpur, I was shaken badly.

"Anywhere around 400 K.M. from Jabalpur in any direction."

Ankush replied not being very precise.

First time in last 15 days since I knew Ankush, today I was finding him behave strangely. Was he trying to be selfish? I do not know why but ever since the posting preferences were being discussed, he was not disclosing with us anything and we expected a lot more from him since he was the only one with existing connection in SBB. Maybe I was overthinking and the pressure under which we all were, made me think madly.

Nobody was interested in studying today and faculties knew this. We were just one of the several batches that they deal with every fortnight, so they knew what we were feeling. It is so strange, how a place which is not our home still has become dearest to our hearts in such a short duration of two weeks.

Rasika was in tears and so were most of the girls in our group. Passing that period till lunch was very difficult that day. In a usual day, we wanted time to pass slowly in SBTC because we enjoyed it thoroughly but today was different. Tension was building and everyone was feeling the heat.

Somehow, we managed to spend half of the day and were at the lunch table. Since it was the last day of our stay, the menu was special today.

"U know I love Pudi Sabji Rasika par aaj ye bhi andar nahi ja rahi."

"Pata nahi kya hi posting milegi."

I said holding her hand in mine.

"I have talked to my uncle let's hope for the best, but even he said the same as Ankush that Jabalpur is full" she said mentioning her connections.

I looked around the dining hall knowing it could well be the last time we were sitting here together eating our food and knowing and realizing that was making it more difficult. Every moment I spent here with Rasika was flashing in my mind.

Soon the lunch was over and unlike other days when after lunch we used to gather in lawn and have fun until we were asked by faculties to join the class, today we all were at our seats in the class even before time.

"There are three RBOs under which you will be assigned, and these are Sagar, Shahdol and Katni."

Even though we knew that Jabalpur was not available, but this confirmation from Daya sir was heart-breaking. We would have loved to be posted at Jabalpur. Ever since I was studying in Jabalpur I wanted to live here, earn here and get settled here and it was even before meeting Rasika.

"Now I will call the names with RBO and you have to come and collect your posting orders." The moment was here when Daya sir was going to announce what we were eagerly waiting for.

"Richi George, Sagar RBO."

Richi was Rasika's friend and she was disappointed since she was also from Jabalpur and Sagar District was opposite for her.

"Shalini Khandelwal Sagar RBO."

Nobody really cared for what Shalini got, maybe only Mridul did.

"Harshita Kaskar Sagar RBO."

Another of her friend was going Sagar.

"Now I also want Sagar RBO. All my friends are going there and since Jabalpur is not an option anymore then it's better to be posted with friends."

Rasika said in a worried tone.

"Don't worry you will get Sagar only."

I replied assuring her.

"Neerja besent Sagar RBO."

Neerja, Harshita, Richi and Rasika were all friends and were a group. Now only Rasika was left, and all others were given same RBO.

"Rasika Agrawal." Sir took a pause and for that moment our hearts also stopped pumping. I desperately wanted her to be posted with her friends but somewhere in my heart I wanted her to be where I was going to be posted. I wanted her to want this too, but she chose her friends over me and I could not express my feelings to her.

"Sagar RBO"

"Finally. Yess!"

Rasika was happy as she collected her order.

"See I told you."

I was also happy for her.

"Yes, you did." She replied cheerfully.

After Rasika, few others were also given Sagar RBO while some of the guys were given Shahdol RBO. My name was not in the list of candidates for Shahdol and I was happy for that since some of the branches of Shahdol RBO were in Singrauli District which was the second most backward district of India. But we never know what plans God has for us. You will see my Singrauli connection in the later part of this story. I never wanted to live in Singrauli specially spending last four years of my life in a city like Jabalpur.

Daya sir continued with his announcements.

"Mridul Ahirwar Katni RBO."

"Ankush Tiwari Katni RBO."

Sir almost called their names jointly like their orders were written combined.

Ankush was not happy with this and even I was shocked listening to this. I was expecting him to be the last candidate to be announced and was sure of being allotted Jabalpur RBO considering his father was also in SBB.

Well his connections are not that strong either I thought in mind.

"Mayank Sharma Katni RBO."

I cannot explain my mixed feelings of listening to these four words. I was happy since I was given my hometown RBO but was equally sad since it was now confirmed that I and Rasika were going to live separately and will work quite far from each other.

Finally, everyone was given their Regional Business Offices (RBO) where we will report the next day which was 31st December 2012.

As our 15-day training in the SBTC facility came to an end, emotions ran high among the 28 new recruits of our batch. Saying goodbye was difficult for all of us, as we had formed strong bonds and friendships during our time together.

Throughout the training, we had worked side by side, learning the ins and outs of banking procedures. We faced challenges together, supported each other through tough times, and celebrated our successes as a team.

As the final day approached, there was a palpable sense of sadness in the air. We realized that we would soon be going our separate ways, going to our respective assignments and duties.

During our farewell gathering, speeches were made, memories were shared, and promises to stay in touch were exchanged. Despite knowing that we would all be moving on to different paths, there was a strong sense of camaraderie among us.

Tears were shed as we hugged each other goodbye, knowing that we had formed a bond that would always remain special to us. We had become more than just colleagues – we had become a family.

Leaving SBTC that day, we carried with us not only the knowledge and skills we had gained during our training, but also the memories of the friendships we had forged. Though we were sad to say goodbye, we were also filled with a sense of pride and accomplishment for having completed the training together.

As we parted ways, we promised to stay connected and support each other in our future endeavors. Though our time together had come to an end, the bonds we had formed would last a lifetime.

Night at the Station

It was 31st December 2012, and I was at Katni RBO with Mridul, Ankush and a few other guys who were allotted Katni. Once the RBO allotment letters were given in SBTC, everyone including me and Rasika left to our homes to spend some time with family since nobody knew where our next place of posting will be. Though I was from Katni, but did not know where the office was located in Katni, thus I took help of Google and found it to be 10 KM away from my home. I took an auto and reached there. We were to report to RBO first and from there the final orders of branches were to be given.

"You are already given home posting bro, you need not to worry."

Ankush said trying to calm my nerves.

"Still, it will be better if they place me at the city centre."

I replied very hopefully.

"Don't expect too much. More often than not, new recruits are given rural branches as their first assignment."

Ankush was giving such matured answers.

We sat quietly waiting outside the main office. Our orders were to be signed by Regional Manager Sir who was the incharge of the whole Katni RBO, administrating more than 50 branches of Swift Bank in nearby cities and villages.

Yesterday when we were allotted RBOs and I came back home, my father introduced me to Gupta uncle. He was an old friend of my father and it was such a coincidence that his son was a trade Union Leader. My name was sent with his recommendation to RBO office already and therefore, I was convinced to get urban posting. This was something I had not shared with any of my friends.

RBO Katni office was the main Regional Office of the bank which administered the nearby branches and staff posting orders for these branches were issued through this office only. The campus of Katni RBO was huge and the main office was inside at the centre with a beautiful garden at front. After staying in SBTC for good 15 days and now this beautiful RBO office, I really started feeling how blessed I was to have been selected and worked in such an institute with great infrastructure.

I reported to RBO at 10 AM sharp in the shivering cold of December and now it was 2 PM and we were still seated outside the office. No sign of our orders yet and we had started feeling hungry.

"Hey babe." What is the status?" Did you get the branch order yet?"

I sent a whatsapp message to Rasika.

Just a day had passed since we left SBTC and I had already started feeling the gap between us.

My phone started ringing and it was her,

"Not yet babu." All the girls are waiting for the same."

"It is getting late and I do not know if we will be able to catch the last train back to Jabalpur."

She replied in a worried tone.

Although Sagar RBO was in opposite direction to that of Jabalpur which was her hometown, but some of the branches that it administered were located nearby Jabalpur as well. So Rasika and her friends were hoping to get those branches allotted. If it happened, then they will have to catch the train back to Jabalpur so that can report to the branch tomorrow.

"Same with us. You know we have been waiting here since morning and they have not even given a clue about place of posting."

I already started to complain, not realizing this was the job I always dreamt of when I was preparing for government jobs. It's funny how we always take things for granted when we have them and forget to cherish their importance. A fortnight ago I would have done anything to get this job and here I was complaining about the work conditions even before joining the branch.

"Bhai lets go and eat something. RBO staff is also having lunch. Maybe after lunch we may get our orders." Mridul asked us all.

There was no canteen inside the RBO but there were small hotels just outside the campus. Mridul took all of us outside the RBO campus. We were hungry but due to excitement and nervousness we had not eaten.

We came back after the lunch and as soon as we entered the premises of RBO, a sub-staff asked us to come to H.R. department. Finally, the moment was here, and my palms were getting sweaty. This was the moment I was waiting for since yesterday.

"Here are the posting orders, but first you guys need to sign here in the register in front of your name."

The pretty H.R. lady asked us to sign on attendance register. Even though we were not working today or the previous 15 days during the training session, but we were officially on duty, and we were being paid for these days as well.

"You are here by ordered to report to Branch manager Barhi Branch immediately after getting this order." I read my order loud.

"Barhi?" I had only heard the name of the place and never been to it. Barhi was a tehsil of Katni and my heart was broken after knowing that I was getting rural posting.

"Barhi mila hai. 50 KM from katni."

I whatsapp Rasika even before informing my parents. For the next ten minutes I was waiting for her to respond but her reply was not received.

"It is the instruction from RM sir that new joining clerks will be posted at rural branches only."

HR manager told us.

We all were disheartened. Even though I was given the closest possible place of posting from my home, but I was still not satisfied with it. Ankush was given Nivar branch which was a very small village of Katni District and was 7 KM from Katni city and was also on railway route and Mridul was given Umaria District. All of us were posted in various districts of Madhya Pradesh only.

"Atleast I will get to see tigers."

Mridul said positively.

"Wo kaise?"

Ankush asked in a jealous tone.

"Bandhavgarh with most tigers in India is in Umaria district only."

I replied knowing the place.

So, after getting to know the place of my posting and not getting any news from Rasika, I left to my home but before going back I made sure to see my friends off to railway station.

I was alone after they were gone and then I called my mother and informed her of getting to post at Barhi branch. She was still happy since I was already living away from last 4 years and distance of Jabalpur, where I was living before joining the bank was 91 KM from Katni whereas Barhi, where I will be working at, is only 50 KM from my home.

It was 8 PM and I had called Rasika for more than 10 times, but it was on my 11th call when she picked up.

"Three of us including Harshita and Vasudha have been given Gotegaon branch."

Rasika informed.

Gotegaon branch was still close to Jabalpur and it also meant that she will pass through Katni while travelling back.

"Where have you been?" I have been calling you since evening and even messaged you but no reply?" You already forgot me?"

I was not concerned about her posting but mad for not replying to my messages and calls, but soon I realized my mistake,

"I am sorry babe but are you alright and have you eaten anything?"

"I am fine and yes we just had dinner."

She replied in her usual cheerful tone.

"When are you going to report to branch?"

"And don't fail to catch your train as it leaves at 10 PM from Sagar."

I asked in anxiety since it was a very cold evening of December, and the last train was leaving in a couple of hours from Sagar to Jabalpur. Tonight, she was going back to Jabalpur, to visit her home with all the girls who were given the same branch.

"Yes, thank you babu for reminding me. We are at the railway station only and going directly to Jabalpur."

Rasika replied very calmly.

"I want to meet you and spend the first day of this new year with you only Rasika." I told her.

"But how is that possible Mayank?"

"I mean we are still at the railway station going to Jabalpur. Then tomorrow we will have to report to branch."

She tried to convince me that it is not the right time to meet. But my desperate and enthusiastic heart could not be convinced, and I said,

"I don't know about tomorrow morning, but I want to spend this New Year night with you."

I just did not want to listen to whatever she was saying.

"I will see you at the station. Your train will reach Katni at 2 AM in the morning and I'll be waiting for you Rasika." My desperation to meet her was at peak.

"Tum pagal ho Mayank." She said and I could feel that she was smiling.

It was still evening, and I had so much time, so I went out and met my childhood friend Brajesh. He was very happy with my selection in SBB and was asking to party with him. He came to pick me up in the evening. This was the time when we did not have any vehicle at our home. I belonged to a lower middle-class family and we were somehow just meeting both the ends.

"Bhai Bhai Bhai many congratulations to you. You deserve it."

Brajesh said while hugging me.

"Thank you bhai. Let's go kya piyega. Aaj ki party meri taraf se."

I was so glad to see him after a long while.

We went out and drank quite a lot and finally when we were done it was getting late.

"Bhai mere sath mere ghar chal. Mummy must have slept; we will sneak in and sleep. I will drop you to station at night when her train arrives."

Brajesh knew I could not go to my home in such drunken state. In Katni our house was having only two small rooms and if someone comes drunk then others sleeping in the same house will come to know. I told Brajesh everything about Rasika and her proposed arrival a night.

But I did not want to bother him especially in such a cold night. It was 11:30 PM and another two and a half hours were left for Rasika's train to reach Katni.

I convinced Brajesh to drop me outside the railways station and I entered the station with hands in my pocket as the temperature in my hometown goes as low as 7°C in the month of December and January. I was only wearing a shirt, since when I left the home, it was only 7 PM and I did not know that I will be spending the night out. It was extremely cold, and this was the time I realized how difficult it would be to spend the time at railway station.

I went straight to the ticket counter and took a platform ticket. At the enquiry counter of railway station, there is a board where they display arrival time and platform in which the train will come. It was a long list of trains, but it did not take me long to identify her train.

"Damn it, platform number one." I read the board.

Her train will come at platform number one, and this was the last thing I wanted.

Platform one is the busiest platform of Katni Railway Station which is directly connected to exit gate, and I was afraid that someone might see me, and I will not be able to explain why I am drunk and at the station at this hour.

Suddenly my phone started to ring and the first thought that hit me it must be Rasika. As soon as I took my phone out, I saw the alarm was buzzing. I had set the alarm for 11:58 PM, so that can call her to wish happy New Year before anyone else. I dialled her number, but it was unreachable. I tried again and again but same was the result every time. It is quite normal inside a moving train to not get the signal. Therefore, I simply messaged her,

"Happy New Year Jaan. I Love You Soooooooo Much."

So, it was 12 AM means officially the New Year 2013 was here and I was sitting alone at the cold bench of katni railway station platform number one in this shivering night.

I was drunk and soon started realizing that we seriously had too much. Brajesh must have slept, and I was finding it difficult to stay awake. I had promised Rasika to receive her when she arrives but staying awake with my condition in the extreme cold was a huge challenge for me. I don't know if it was the alcohol or the cold night that I could not keep my eyes open. I thought I will just lie down to relax my body and mind a little.

Cold was at its peak and temperature was going down with every passing hour. I did not have anything to cover and protect myself from this chilly winter night. I simply took my handkerchief out and tied it like a mask which covered my nose and ears. This stopped cold air to enter through ears.

My mother always says nose and ears if covered stop half the cold.

I still do not remember how and when but even after resisting to the maximum of my abilities, I slept. Never in this world I wanted to sleep that night, but I did.

I do not know for how long I slept but I woke up with the vibration of phone. As soon as I tried to take my phone out a shock hit me. My phone was not in my pocket and the first thing I thought shit, someone must have picked it as it is so common to lose your valuables at railway station. But wait a minute did I not just wake hearing the mobile phone sound and vibration.

I looked thoroughly and there was my phone just beneath the bench I was sleeping. I thanked God since I could not afford to lose my phone for two reasons. First, I could not afford to buy one immediately as I had not enough money and second, without a phone I will not be able to contact Rasika which was way more important at that moment.

I picked it up and saw 13 miscalls and all were from Rasika. It was 2:15 AM already and her train was to come at 2 AM.

I was sure that her train must have left since the stoppage of the train was only 10 minutes in Katni station, and I was cursing myself for sleeping. She must be mad at me.

I looked around and realized that a train was already at the platform and while I was lost deep in my thoughts again my phone started ringing and it was Rasika.

I picked it up,

"Where are you?" My train is at the Katni station."

Rasika was furious at the other side.

"just 2 minutes and I will be at your seat."

I replied cheerfully knowing I had not missed her train.

I ran and reached to S7 which she had earlier informed me about and entered the couch.

"Aa gaya mayank finally. Hame to laga tum nahi aoge."

Her friend Richi who was also travelling to Jabalpur said to me.

"Sharma ji kabhi wade se nahi mukarte."

Rasika defended me as always and I hugged her.

"I love you Rasika and I am so sorry I slept; I did not know when. I tried to call you at 12 AM to wish you New Year, but your phone was unreachable."

I tried to express all the mixed feelings and guilt that I was going through.

"Shhh..."

"Happy New Year Babu" and she kissed me on cheeks in front of everyone.

"Happy new year Rasika."

I was the happiest person in the world at that moment. 10 minutes ago, I was cursing myself that maybe I ruined the moment and now here I was with my dream girl.

We said goodbye to everyone and stepped out of the train.

It was actually crazy of me to ask her to spend the night together when actually I did not have any place to go. I just wanted to spend the time with her even if it meant spending it at the railway station.

"Let's go find some hotel Mayank it is way too cold. How did you manage this long just in a shirt?"

She wanted to go to a hotel and being a guy how could I resist but still I denied for other reasons.

"We can't. Someone might see us. It's way too risky Rasika. People know me and it will be difficult to explain na."

"jaisa aap kahen babu."

She said smiling and acknowledging my decency. I mean no guy in the world will deny getting a cozy bed in such a cold night with a girl as hot as Rasika, but I did.

As she was travelling in a sleeper class, so was having a bed sheet and blanket as railway does not provide it. We took that out from her bag and spread it at a cleaner part of the platform and sat over it and further took the blanket over us.

It was the best feeling ever. The warmth of the blanket and her love was enough to make me feel comfortable.

"Bahut achha lag rha hai" I said looking in her eyes.

"I feel the same." She replied with all the love in her eyes.

"I wonder how you managed to stay alive just in a shirt for last three hours." She asked.

"Well I am born hot you know."

I tried to flirt with her and she smiled. It is maybe the secret of happy life and relationship with your loved ones. You need not to change your behaviour just because you have her now. She needs to be treated all the same and special always.

I could not resist and while we were lost deep in each other's eyes we kissed as the platform was almost empty, and nobody was around us. It was a short kiss followed by another short one then our lips parted and the soft feeling of her tongue in my mouth and then it was a play that we used to play with my tongue trying to catch her with my lips opened.

"I love you Rasika. I really love you and cannot live without you." I expressed my love to her.

"I love you too." She replied in between the kisses while looking in my eyes.

We wanted that moment to freeze while we sat there hugging under the blanket. It was 4 in the morning of 1st January 2013 and the platform was almost empty.

I still remember each and every detail. Maybe because I got to spend this beautiful moment with her after those difficult 3 hours alone at the platform. Rewards that we get after such hardship are the most cherished ones and I was realizing it now.

Soon the night was almost over, and it was time for her to go to Jabalpur.

"I will not report to branch today. I will sleep the whole day since none of my friends are reporting to branch today."

Rasika said in a sleepy tone when we were buying her ticket to Jabalpur.

"Bye I will miss you badly."

I said hugging her one last time before she left.

I had planned to safely spend some time with her and see her off early morning so that no one can notice what has just happened.

She waved at me standing at the gate while her train left the platform.

It was 5:30 in the morning of New Year and I thought it still is too early to go home. I had told my mother that will spend the night at Brajesh's place.

Finally, after spending the whole night at the station I came outside with a smile on my face and a mixed feeling of excitement and nervousness of officially going to work for the first time in my life. Once I came out of the railway station, I bought a Center Fresh and started chewing it. I could not take risk and let my parents know with my breath that I had consumed alcohol.

CHAPTER IV

Embracing Office Life

It was 1st January 2013, 7 AM in the morning and I was ready to go to office for my first day.

"Mayank dahi shakkar rakha hai kha ke hi jana aur bhagwan ko hath jod lo."

My mother told me.

"Han mummy." I replied while brushing my hair.

Even without looking at her I knew the emotions she was going through. She has spent last 22 years raising me and making me who I am today. Her immense hard work and support for my studies even in extremely difficult period of economic crisis has resulted in today and she was really proud of me. Even after 10 years writing it today my eyes are wet thinking about her sacrifices. She belonged to a wealthy family but somehow after marriage she went through a difficult period of more than 2 decades. All I wanted was to give her a good life, a decent house and peace of mind that she deserved.

I left for the railway station in hurry since only one train directly goes to Barhi from Katni and I did not want to miss that.

Papa came to station with me and since station is not away from our home we chose to walk. My relationship with my father is something I cannot explain easily. We do not talk much, nor do we spend much time together but still the love and respect I feel for him is unmatchable. Relation between a father and son is often not very expressive. Yes, we fail to tell each other how much we care and how much I wanted to hug him that day, but we did not. It is like that between us from the beginning and unfortunately it will go on. I really wish someday I will be able to hug my father and mummy because ever since I remember things, I have never hugged them.

"Train aa rahi hai 6 number platform par mayank."

Papa said after giving me tickets that he bought.

"Han papa ab aap jaiye mai chala jaunga."

I said this and left to enter the platform.

My train arrived on time and I hopped into it. Seats were empty since this route to Barhi was not the main railway route and trains as well as number of passengers were quite limited.

I sat at the side window seat and as the seat in front of me was empty, I relaxed myself and spread the legs. I took out my phone, connected the wired earphones and played "Aadat" by Jal the band. This was my favourite song and it still is. No matter what the situation is or what or how I am feeling, but I will always play this song. Music has such healing effect and all you need to do is find the one that works for you.

Barhi is only 50 KM from Katni and it took one and a half hour for train to reach there. Train arrived at Barhi

Station at 9:45 AM and I took an auto to bank. I was in hurry as I have always been a punctual guy and never wanted to be late on my first day to work.

Auto driver stopped just in front of the bank. I stepped out of auto, gave him 80 Rs and paused for a moment and looked thoroughly. It was an old building having this old glow shine board with an ATM and crowd outside the bank premises. Gate was about to open and I along with customers waited for it to open.

Guard opened the gate and people who were standing outside, rushed in as everyone wanted to be the first person in line of cash deposit/withdrawal counter.

I entered the premises after all the customers got inside. I was to report to the branch manager of Barhi branch, so I looked for his cabin. His cabin was close to the entry gate and thus I did not have any difficulty in finding it, but to my surprise it was empty.

"Branch Manager Sir has not yet arrived."

A tall dark but not so handsome guy in his white shirt told me.

"I am new staff here." I told him realizing that he was a sub-staff.

"Arey sahab where are you from? I am Dayaram, Daftari of this branch."

He said smiling at me.

I was impressed with his tone as it had both respect and warmth.

"I am from Katni only Dayaram."

I replied to him smiling back.

"Branch manager sir usually comes late let me take you to the accountant sahab."

He took me to the cabin of accountant.

Mr. Suresh Deovanshi was the accountant of the branch. He was an old man with only 6 years of service left as I came to know that later.

"Good Morning sir, I am Mayank Sharma new SWO-I."

I greeted him while introducing myself. Single Window Operator or SWO is the designation of clerks working in government banks.

"Good Morning Sharma Ji." Deovanshi sir greeted back.

"Ye sahab bhi Katni se hi hain sir."

Dayaram introduced me to Deovanshi sir as he was also from Katni. The old accountant was quite slow in replies and took all the time in the world to respond. He took my branch reporting order and asked Dayaram to get a Xerox of it.

"What are your qualifications Mayank Ji?"

Asked Deovanshi sir.

"I have done B. Com Computers sir."

I replied hesitantly.

"Let's get your ID created and then you can start working. Where will you like to work? I mean cash counter or transfer counter?" He further asked about my preference.

"Sir I have no idea so whatever task you think fits me; I am willing to work." I replied being positive for all sorts of work.

"Mayank ji come let me first introduce you to other staff members."

Deovanshi sir took me for the tour of the branch. Though during training, we were given a branch visit to understand how a typical branch of a PSU bank runs, but one understands it properly when he actually starts to work in it.

First of all, I was taken to the Cash counter. There were two counters for cash, one was for Cash Deposit and the other was Cash Withdrawal counter.

Saraiya ji was the Cash Officer of the branch and was sitting at Deposit Counter.

He seemed to be a very kindhearted person as positive vibe was coming from him along with the smell of alcohol. Jitendra Meena sir was sitting in withdrawal counter and he was the smart one, I guess.

I greeted both of them and since large numbers of customers were in queue, I was just able to introduce myself to them and the conversation was short. Then I was shown cheque transfer counter which was empty and at last there was a passbook printing counter.

"Both of our clerks are engaged in cash counters whole day then after 4 PM when the gate is closed, Meena ji takes care of transfer vouchers and other customer service requests such as change of mobile number, entry of ATM cards and several other things that you will gradually come to know when you sit here."

Deovanshi sir explained me.

Next was the passbook printing counter and someone was printing all the passbooks of the customers who were standing in a long line.

"He is Mishra ji Mayank and Mishra Ji this is Mayank; he has joined today."

Deovanshi sir introduced me to him and I said Namaste. As he was also busy with the bundle of passbooks, I only had formal interaction with him. Next, I was shown credit department and met credit incharge.

"I already knew about your posting Mayank."

Credit Incharge sir seemed happy while shaking my hand and welcomed me. I had met all the staff except my Branch Head, and he had just arrived, so Deovanshi sir took me to his cabin.

"Sir Mayank Sharma has reported today." Deovanshi sir once again introduced me.

"Welcome to SBB Sharma." Kaise aaye train or bus?"

He asked looking very carefully at me.

"Sir I came by train since I did not know about the bus route."

I replied while looking at him.

Mr. Babulal Labade was my first branch manager and I still remember him exactly as he was. He was a very senior officer with only 3 years of service left. I now noticed that I was the youngest guy in the office and all other were near or above 40 years of age.

"Sir I will now send application form to RBO for creation of ID so that Mr. Mayank can start working."

"Till the ID is created let's sit him at the passbook printing counter."

Said Deovanshi sir.

"Okay all the best Sharma." Said my branch manager and I smiled back thanking him.

At one time or another, whatever the post or seat you may get in future, in a PSU bank you will surely be given an opportunity to sit at the passbook counter. Printing passbook was new to me and since I was only using ATM for withdrawals and balance information when I was living in Jabalpur for studies, I did not realize the importance of passbook printing in banks for customers.

"Mishra Ji teach Mayank Ji how to print passbooks."

Deovanshi sir instructed Mishra Ji as I was given the counter for today.

"Other than passbooks, customer requests will also be given to you in this counter Mayank Ji. Just make sure that mobile number is also written in the application and is attached with an ID proof."

Mishra ji was trying to explain the responsibilities of staff sitting in this counter.

"In the passbook counter you are given a passbook by the customer. Enter the account number mentioned on the passbook in the system and verify the name first. If you type wrong account number, then someone else's number will be displayed and if not looked carefully mistakes will happen."

“Therefore, once you verify the name, click on proceed and system will show you the last entry that was printed on passbook and you have to open the last printed page on passbook and match the dates. It must be the same date as shown in the system. More often than not the dates are same and then you have to enter this side up into the printer and just press okay.”

Passbook printer started to make it’s unique sound and passbook was completely gone inside the printer and in a few seconds, it came out. I checked the passbook and the latest entry of cash deposit was printed on it.

“When it is successfully printed just give it back to the customer and go for the next one.”

Mishra Ji guided me thoroughly. I was impressed with his expertise and the way he was explaining things to me. When I first looked at him while he was introduced by Deovanshi sir, I made a judgement about him to be a typical government babu since his attire was such. He wore a ‘Gamchha’, chewing Paan all the time and spitting. I thought he must only be passing time, but now I was realizing why a book must not be judged by its cover.

I found the whole process very amusing and took the passbook from next customer and repeated the procedure exactly as explained to me by Mishra Ji and it worked. I felt so happy printing first passbook of my life without any hassles.

“Aap kijiye ham aate hain.”

Mishra Ji gave me full access to the counter after realising that I was able to print it and went outside to have some refreshments. For him, it was an opportunity to relax while I was finding it very entertaining as it was my first day at the office.

Half of the day was already over, and it was five past 2 PM and I heard Head Cashier screaming,

"Close the gate guard sahab. It's already lunch time."

PSU banks lunch time jokes were not yet famous back then.

Since no further entries were allowed for next half an hour of lunch, Mishra Ji asked the customers to come after lunch.

Even though I left home early in the morning, my mother as always had packed my lunch.

The unconditional love of a mother is something one can never find in any other person in life. Some realize it at the early stage of their life while others do it later.

"Sahab lets go inside near the canteen room. Lunch table is there."

Dayaram told me about the place where we can have lunch. As I entered the place, I saw that none of the other staff members were there and I found it strange. I had my lunch along with Mishra Ji who happily shared his food with me.

"Baki sahab log ghar jaate hain khane aur manager sahab and Deovanshi ji take it in their cabins."

Mishra Ji informed me knowing my puzzled face.

I finished my lunch and sat back at the counter and it was not yet 2:30 PM.

"Had lunch babe?"

I sent a whatsapp message to Rasika. I was feeling hesitant to use my mobile phone since it was instructed in a board not to use mobile phone inside the branch. Later I realized that it was for customers and not for staff. How foolish of me right?

"I had brunch babu and you? How is the first day at branch? I just woke up half an hour ago."

Her reply came after a few minutes.

Rasika was sleeping ever since she reached home and she along with other girls had decided to report to branch tomorrow. They had already informed the respective branches about the late reporting.

The gate was opened and once again at 2:30 PM I saw the repetition of morning ritual of people pushing each other to get inside the branch before others. In less than a minute the branch which was empty with pindrop silence a few moments ago was now heavily crowded and all the counters including mine were packed with customers and work.

I was quite slow in printing passbook initially and the reason was obvious as I was new, but I liked how customers were standing patiently for their turn to come.

"Aram se kariye sahab ye log pralay aane tak khade rahenge passbook ke lie."

Mishra Ji sarcastically spoke in a low voice. Such is the charisma of a passbook. First day lesson that I learnt was print their passbooks and they will never complain.

Soon it was 4 PM and the gate was closed again. Cash counter was closed, and several customers were still inside the bank. Saraiya Ji was shouting at the guard for letting people in even after 4 PM while customers were saying that they came before 4.

"Ye to roz ka jhagda hai Mayank sir." Mishra Ji told me.

All this while one thing that I noticed was how smoothly Meena Ji ran his counter. Not a single customer was complaining about not getting his withdrawal.

It was now 5 PM and I also wanted to go home since Mishra Ji had already picked his bag and left.

I asked Dayaram how to reach Katni from Barhi at this time and he informed that the last bus leaves at 5:45. I went to the cabin of accountant since branch manager was not in his cabin, and informed that I will leave now since I have to go back to Katni.

"You better take a room here as everyday up down is quite difficult."

Deovanshi sir told me that he was also from Katni but only goes home on weekends as it gets late in bank during weekdays.

"Yes, I will sir, but until I find a place to live here in Barhi, I will need to go back to Katni daily."

I was permitted and I ran with my bag towards the bus stop and luckily the location of our branch was very close to it. It only took me 2 minutes to reach there and I finally caught the last bus. I made a reminder to anyhow leave the office before 5:30 PM to smoothly catch the bus.

It took an hour and half for bus to reach Katni bus stand and from there I took an auto till auto stand and then walked back to home.

It was 7:45 and I was at home feeling very happy to have completed my first day at work.

"Kaisa tha din Mayank?"

"Chai banayen?"

Asked my mother as she was extremely happy, and her happiness was visible from her face.

I explained my mother about the whole day and working of the branch.

Resting in bed sipping tea, I had a long chat with Rasika. Since my house was too small having no privacy, I could not call her and therefore we were chatting the whole time. Next morning, I had to catch the bus at 8 in the morning to reach office on time, so I took an early dinner and slept.

Unexpected Company

Next morning, I woke up at 6 AM without any alarm and felt really fresh. After getting ready and having breakfast, I went out and took an auto till Gayatri Mandir and then changed another auto to reach the bypass road from where I will catch the bus to Barhi. Though there was an easier route to catch the bus at the Katni Bus Stand, but for catching the same bus from the bus stand, I will need to go an hour earlier, so I preferred this route.

I was waiting at the bypass for the bus to arrive. Since it was my first day to catch the bus, I did not know the exact location where the bus will stop. There was no proper bus stop or any sign and all I could do was ask Pan Waale Bhaiya the whereabouts of the bus to Barhi.

In India, Paan Waala will always know everything about anything and more often than not his information is correct.

At last my bus arrived at 8:30 AM and luckily it was not fully crowded, and I got a seat.

"Barhi 1 ticket." I said to the conductor.

I paid 60 Rs for my ticket to the conductor of the bus and immediately calculated 120 Rs for bus and 60 Rs for two ways auto daily. Spending 180 Rs every day only for travel seemed a bit too much for a guy like me who used to manage all his living expenses within 5000 per month in a city like Jabalpur. Here I was spending more than that just in travelling. I made my mind to find a house in Barhi as soon as possible since daily up down was an expensive affair.

Three days had passed since I joined the branch and I was still travelling to Barhi from katni daily by bus.

"Meena ji how much will my first salary be?"

I asked Meena Ji while we were closing the cash after remitting it to Cash Officer Saraiya Ji. Though we were told about the approximate monthly gross salary during our last day class at SBTC, but I still wanted to confirm from Meena sir who also was a clerk but was working in higher capability.

"Bhai with your basic it will be anywhere around Rs 14000 initially."

Meena ji replied while tying the bundle of 500 Rs Note.

My mind immediately started to calculate if I will be able to save anything with this salary as I will also have to provide to my mother. I had asked Dayaram and all other staff to help me in getting a room in Barhi. My uncle also had some contacts in Barhi and he informed me about a house of his friend which was located close to my branch.

Since I did not have any vehicle and I surely did not want to spend on auto, getting a place at walking distance from my branch was my preferred choice. I was taken to the proposed room after office by the son of the landlord. The place was having two rooms and unlike big cities, here you will not find any privacy since rooms are small in size and adjacent to rooms where other tenants and owner's family live.

"Our daughter is also working in a PSU bank."

Said the landlord.

My landlord was having an electrical shop at the Barhi main market. They were a family of 5 having two daughters and a son with parents. The eldest daughter was working while the younger one was preparing for exams after completing her graduation and yes, she was pretty. I thought days will pass smoothly here so I said yes to the room. They gave me the keys since I was a known to them at least this is what I thought. Rent for the room was Rs 1500 per month and I felt it was genuine. The only problem with the room was not having an attached washroom. Separate washroom for person living in this room was provided on the first floor which basically was the terrace of the house.

As soon as I called and informed Saraiya Ji about the place that I have got on rent he smiled and said,

"Badhiya jagah lie hain room Sharma Ji."

I could not understand the meaning of his sarcastic comment at that moment but later I heard from most of my colleagues that beautiful mother and daughter duo was famous in Barhi. The landlady was having a famous affair with previous branch head of my branch and the same room was being used by him during his tenure in Barhi.

I felt strange at that moment since I had just met Rasika and did not want to spoil what was being developed between us, but with the distance and ever shortening time that we spent talking to each other, will this homestay create any hurdle or will she ever be able to know if something happened. Several such thoughts were going in my mind.

I had not yet started living in that house and my sinister mind was already thinking the worst possibilities. I do not know if this is with every guy, but I start imagining things and imaginations have no limits.

So next day when I came from Katni, I took a bag along to move in the famous house which was rented. That particular day I was finding it difficult to pass the time at branch as I wanted to go to room and see myself if the rumours were true and the ladies were as I was told.

It was 5:30 PM and I came out of office and walked back. Soon I reached the place and keyed in and opened the door of my room and first time I looked carefully at everything. It was a naked room with no furniture at all and I did not even have a bed to sleep so I thought to ask the landlord for the same. It was still the first week of January and the winter was at its peak.

"Hi Jaan."

I called Rasika and she was in train with other girls as they used to travel back to Jabalpur every day after office.

"Hi babu room aa gaye?" "How is it? How are you feeling?" I miss you badly babu."

She asked knowing that I had got the room.

"I miss you more jaan. It is alright but I do not have a bed here and it is quite cold."

"When will you reach Jabalpur? And when will we meet next? I really want to meet and hug you. It's been long since I even touched you Rasika." I fired all my emotions at her.

"I am about to reach Narsinghpur then another hour from there till I reach home."

"Why are you speaking in such a low voice Mayank?"

She asked noticing it.

"Well! There are three reasons of that." I replied.

"And what are they may I know Mr. Sharma?" She asked in a funny yet cute tone.

"First of all, it is very cold, and I badly miss the warmth of your body." I started flirting.

"Someone is trying to be romantic."

She said.

"Second I feel very lonely here."

"And third is I can't speak loud even if I want to since everything, I say can easily be heard by the others living in adjacent rooms. This place is small and echoing voice in winters is just like cherry on cake, easily noticed. You want neighbours to know about our secrets?"

We were talking our hearts out but suddenly her voice started to break, and we had to hang up. It always happened and I felt very disappointed and lonely since I was new to this place and did not know anyone. In a cold evening with no one to talk and moreover no bed to sleep, I felt like the loneliest person in the world. I was hungry and wanted to eat something, so I wore my jacket and went out in my flip flops.

It is amazing that cities or even a village completely changes itself as soon as the sun goes down. People, roads and building everything seemed different or maybe I was looking at them differently. During the daytime I was always in hurry and hardly had time to take a thorough look at things but now I could take a pause and observe things. People mostly wore rural attire and I started getting the vibes of living in a village. The air was colder than it was a couple of hours ago when I came home. There were not many food stalls or shops and most of them were either selling Samosa chat or roasted peanuts. In order to reach to the main market, I had to pass through a narrow lane first then a comparatively dark patch of the road where most people were sitting with their bottles of local liquor which smelled very tangy. Even from a fair distance I could smell alcohol nevertheless, I kept walking and reached to the more populated stretch of the road and it was the same place where I usually take bus to Katni. I came here because it was the only place where I could eat decent food in Barhi also the owner of the place was a friend of my uncle.

I ordered dal fry, paneer and chapati with butter and sat there observing the place. Yes, it was a Pure vegetarian restaurant. This is the same ritual for all vegetarians. They spend good 15 minutes scanning the menu and at last this is what they mostly order. It seemed like a newly built restaurant as the furniture was new. Place was having regular customers and thus I hoped that the restaurant would be offering good food.

My father always says "Jis chat ke thele mein bheed ho wahan adhiktar chat achhi milegi."

It does not mean that my father liked samosa chat, it is just the way he explained things. He knows everything about everything and is also the most knowledgeable person that I have personally met and known.

My order arrived and it looked good and the taste was equally good. I finished it quickly since the time was passing fast and I had to walk back through the same scary lane again and the other issue was I still had to manage my beddings for tonight.

I walked pass the same lane quickly and this time did not look at the people there and soon reached my room. I unlocked the door and entered the house. It was 9:30 PM and all the lights of the building were off, and I could not hear anyone either which meant everyone was already asleep. My plan was to ask the landlady to help me with the bedding tonight and then from tomorrow I will somehow manage but it failed. I was wearing a jacket and was only having a thin bed sheet and the temperature was falling further with every passed minute. Now I knew nothing could be done, so I had to survive this night without any bed. I laid on the bed sheet wearing my jacket and placed my office bag beneath the head. I plugged in the headphone and played "Aadat."

"Good Night Jaan."

I messaged Rasika and closed my eyes. I was feeling cold and tired and since nothing was under my control, I was trying to sleep and somehow pass this extremely cold night.

I do not remember if I slept or not but in the stillness of the night, a knock echoed through the quiet corridor. There was a knock on my door and when I opened it, I saw the daughter of my landlord stood at the doorway, a blanket in hand, offering solace from the chilly air. As she entered, it became apparent that she was in her early twenties, much like me, and harbored a certain fondness for me.

The daughter, whose name I was yet to learn, initiated a conversation as she handed me the blanket.

"Hi you must be Mayank." She said while continuously looking in my eyes.

"Hello. Yes, and you are?" I was confused, excited and was feeling the cold.

"I am Reena. I live here with my parents."

While she introduced herself, I remembered that I knew her name already from the first conversation with her mother.

"I know you're the new tenant here. I saw you did not come here with much of luggage and winters in Barhi can be really harsh, so my mother sent me to help you." She was very cheerful and helping in nature.

"Can I come in? It's freezing out here." She wanted to come inside.

Now until this moment I was acting like a Sakht Launda but yahan mai pighal gaya.

"Sure."

I allowed her to come into my room alone at very late hours of this amazing night.

Let's try to understand the scenario. I landed in this small tehsil a couple of days ago for the first time in my life. I rented this room yesterday and met this girl just 15 minutes ago whose parents were sleeping right beside my room and here she was inside my room and the clock said it was 12:30 AM. I already had heard stories about the ladies of this house and here I was stuck in this situation even after knowing everything.

I did not even have any chair in my room or mat either and since it was extremely cold, the only place where we could sit was the bed sheet on which I was earlier lying. Realizing the scene inside the room she sat on the bed sheet and asked me to sit too. After all she was the owner of the house and I was just a young tenant.

Now I carefully watched her; she was wearing a small night suit which was not covering her legs completely. She sat and bent towards me and it showed her assets quite well. By this time, I knew her intentions, but I could not help looking at her. A couple of hours ago I was cursing my luck feeling alone and now I was about to become one of the luckiest guys of Barhi. She was indeed beautiful and hot as well.

The situation became increasingly ambiguous for me, when I found myself torn between acknowledging her advances and maintaining the boundaries of professionalism and personal commitment.

Committed to a relationship with Rasika, I confronted a moral dilemma in navigating the unexpected advances of my landlord's daughter at this time of the night.

As the conversation unfolded, Reena's flirtatious gestures escalated, leaving me confused, how to navigate in this crucial situation. The boundary between a friendly exchange and an inappropriate advance blurred, challenging my willpower to uphold the principles of fidelity and commitment to Rasika.

In a moment of clarity, I recognized the need to create boundaries and prioritize the loyalty that I owed to Rasika. Despite the tempting situation, I decided to interrupt the trajectory of the interaction. With my ethical responsibility, I requested Reena to leave, emphasizing the importance of maintaining a professional and respectful atmosphere. I did not want to leave any such impression specially since it was my first day in this house.

"It's already 2:15 Reena don't you have to sleep?" I asked.

"I sleep quite late, but do you want me to go?" She replied.

"Well ofcourse not." I really was not sure what I really wanted.

We talked for a bit about our lives and about so many things. She told me about her future aspirations and while talking I did realize that she was holding my hand the whole time. Suddenly my phone beeped, and it was a message from Rasika. She had reached home and was going to sleep. This was the moment when I came in my senses. Realizing the sudden change of expression on my face she left and yes, we exchanged our numbers. Once she was gone, I realised that I was fortunate enough to avoid something which could have destroyed my relationship.

The Counter Job

"Priyanka Upadhyay"

"Yes sir" the lady in front of my counter replied.

"The mobile number linked to my account has been lost sir, so I want to change my number."

"Please attach your Aadhaar card or any other identity proof with the application and write full account number with your signature on both the application and ID proof."

I replied to one of the customers without even looking at her.

"But sir I have only brought the originals and not the Xerox of my Aadhaar."

She tried to convince me.

"Alright let me see your Aadhaar."

First time I looked at her and she was pretty. I cursed myself for not looking at the face earlier. I should go to hell for the sin that I have committed.

I verified her Aadhaar with the portal and once convinced I said,

"Okay Priyanka I will now change your mobile number. It will be effective from tomorrow and meanwhile you can download our mobile banking app for all the banking facilities."

She kept looking at me and longer than normal eye contact was unusual for me. Both of us smiled and then she left.

So, my days were passing nicely you can imagine. I was given the counter for all miscellaneous works. My job was to receive application for change of mobile number, nominee change in savings account, open fixed deposit-recurring deposit account, KYC updation, opening of account, selling PAI (Personal Accidental Insurance), to activate the dormant or freezed accounts and issuing ATM card. With such variety of works I was engaged the whole day with one task or another.

After changing mobile number of Priyanka, I wrote transaction number on the application, signed and sealed it then gave it to an officer who sat behind me. Once a clerk does anything, his work must be verified by an officer and only then the job will be performed completely.

I made a note to look at every customer of my counter and smile at them as it will make them feel good and yes, I will not miss any pretty face.

"Sir my son wants to open an account, but he does not have a PAN card yet."

I looked and smiled at the person appealing to me. He was a man in his late 40s and was accompanied by a boy who I assumed to be below 18 years of age. When I was going to study in Jabalpur, I along with my uncle had visited a branch of SBB and even the branch manager was known to my uncle, yet my account was not opened just because I did not have a PAN card. But bank policy does not restrain a minor to open his/her account anywhere in India. I was not aware of the fact when I was to open my account and ultimately, I had to visit a private bank for opening of account and it was quite difficult to arrange minimum balance that they require for a savings account. Today I saw someone in the similar situation, and I was determined to help him here. Usually I never accept account opening forms directly from customers and just open the forms received by any officer, but today I took the initiative and filled all the mandatory fields and when it was completely filled, I got it verified for opening.

"Here is your ATM card and internet banking kit sir. Account number and passbook will be issued shortly, please have a seat."

I gave him the kit and both the father and son were happy and thankful to me. On discussing further with them, I came to know that the boy was going to study in Indore and his father will send monthly pocket money through this account only. They were also astonished to experience such quality of banking service from a government bank.

It did not take me long to have his account number generated and soon I issued them the passbook also.

"Here is your passbook. All the best."

I gave him the passbook and smiled. I was extremely happy and satisfied and it was something I had never felt earlier. I realised why they say to help people. Not only it is morally good but the inner joy you feel is unmatchable. This lesson was the biggest take away for me today.

The Australian Couple

In the serene landscape of a village like Barhi, a government bank stands as a pillar of financial support for the locals. One fine day, I did not know that my proficiency in English would bridge cultural gaps and leave an indelible mark on the hearts of an Australian couple.

It was a typical day in Barhi village, where the hustle and bustle of city life seemed like a distant memory. The bank, surrounded by lush green fields and a sense of community, served as a lifeline for the villagers. On this particular day, an Australian couple, seeking to withdraw money from our ATM, found themselves in a difficult situation. The local bank guard struggled to communicate with them, as English was not his forte.

ATM Guard was trying his best to communicate with them and understand their issue. In a village like Barhi, foreigners are seen as someone coming from a different planet. Good number of people had gathered around our ATM and since branch manager had access to the CCTV screen, noticing this scenario, he asked the branch accountant to see why there were so many people gathered around our ATM. To investigate the issue, our accountant, Mr. Deovanshi, went outside and saw the Australian couple having problem with their withdrawal. Even though the accountant sir was senior but to my surprise, he was also not well versed with the

English Language. He tried a bit and then sent a sub-staff to bring me.

"Accountant sir has called you to come to the ATM immediately sir."

Sub-staff informed me.

I stopped the counter work and went outside. Untill then I was not aware of the developments happening in ATM.

"What is the matter sir?"

I asked humbly not being aware of what was happening.

"They are having trouble while withdrawing the money Sharma ji try to understand their problem."

My accountant tried to explain me about the situation.

"Hello sir. How may I help you? I work here in this branch and this ATM is maintained by us."

I asked the gentleman.

He was around 6"3 tall, white and must be in his early 50s and his wife was short and on the heavier side. Both of them looked troubled and were sweating badly.

"Hello! We are from Australia and were going to Bandhavgarh for Tiger Safari. We ran out of cash and have tried several ATMs, but none is working. I still have to make several payments. I don't know how I'm going to manage that."

He explained me the actual cause of his trouble.

I looked at his card and it was not an ATM card, atleast not the kind of cards we use in ATMs regularly.

"Have you ever withdrawn cash using this card anywhere in India before?"

I enquired.

"I don't remember withdrawing cash using this card from any ATM machine, but I have used this at exchange counter, and they gave me Indian Currency using this card."

He replied.

"In my opinion this card will not allow you to withdraw cash directly from ATM machines sir. You will have to visit the nearest exchange centre which is located in Bandhavgarh only. From there only you can get Indian Currency by swiping this card."

I narrated him the solution.

"Ahh so that is the reason. I must be confused then. Thank you so much."

The couple thanked me again and again.

I have been to Bandhavgarh earlier which is a well-known Tiger Reserve of Central India and have seen the exchange centre as numerous foreigners visit the place regularly. I explained the route to their driver and asked him to help them as they are our guests in India.

UPI was not introduced back then, and cash was majorly used for most of the payments. My proficiency in English was an uncommon skill in the rural setting. I guided the couple through their financial transaction.

The incident did not go unnoticed by my branch manager, who was both surprised and delighted by exceptional service. Labade sir, impressed by my ability to connect with customers from different cultural backgrounds, recognized the importance of such qualities in the ever-expanding globalized world.

Beyond the immediate impact on the Australian couple, my actions had a lasting effect on the reputation of the bank. The incident also prompted the bank to invest in language training for its employees. Recognizing the changing dynamics of the global economy, the management understood the need for its staff to be equipped with the skills necessary to navigate diverse linguistic landscapes. My experience became a catalyst for positive change within the organization.

My Encounter with Abundance

More than a week had already passed since I started working in Barhi branch and I was enjoying my job. It was a Wednesday which is mid of the week and customer count is comparatively low on Wednesday and Thursday in banks.

"Sharma ji chaliye aaj apko Cash counter ka experience dilwate hain."

Deovanshi sir came to my counter and told me to have experience of the work at Cash Counter also.

"Sure sir." I replied positively.

I closed my counter and put all the pending applications in my drawer and went along with him.

"There are two Cash Counters, one is for deposit and the other is for withdrawal. Withdrawal counter is relatively easier to operate here since bulk deposit is difficult to manage as it requires speed to count huge money and you also have to sort the notes then and there."

Deovanshi sir explained to me.

"Sir rather get him seated in deposit counter only since he is new and if excess payment is given to any customer it will create trouble."

Saraiya sir who was the cash officer told Deovanshi sir.

"Okay then Saraiya ji carry on with him and be seated here with him and guide him."

He said and left to his cabin.

"He is a slow poison be very careful with him."

It was Saraiya ji's view about Deovanshi sir and I just listened and smiled without reacting.

I entered the cash counter which was locked from inside and only the Cashier had the key. It means without his permission; nobody can enter the counter which is actually very important since cash counter is the most sensitive area of a bank branch. I looked carefully and noticed that it was a small counter filled with one small note counting machine, one giant machine with three layers which not only counts the money but also sorts the soiled notes. There was a magnifier and a small heater also on the counter just beside the computer.

"Saraiya sir, what is this heater doing here taking space in this already small counter?"

I asked curiously to him who laughed at my question and replied,

"This is not a heater but ultraviolet lazer to check if the currency note is real or fake as it emits blue light."

He answered while smiling at me and showing how it worked.

There was something which made me feel nice about this guy. Only positive vibe came from him even though he remained drunk most of the times, but his heart was pure.

At the miscellaneous counter job, there was no specific pattern of the tasks that I performed, but here in cash counter I had to follow the procedure in certain manner. When a customer comes to the counter, he will give a deposit slip along with the money that he wishes to deposit. Before counting money, I have to read the deposit slip carefully. Account number must be written clearly, and complete 13-digit account number should be written along with the name of the account holder. Then the next step was to check and calculate the note details. The last thing was to make sure customer has signed the deposit slip along with mobile number. Mobile number comes very useful when there are problems with the deposited notes or amount or account number. After verifying and calculating the details on deposit slip the next step is to actually count the money.

Just imagine you have deposited certain amount of money in the bank but the account number written on the slip is not a valid number or it belongs to someone else or in other case the name you have written does not match with the mentioned account number. What will a cashier do in such situation? Where will the money go in the evening when cash counter is closed? If there is mobile number on the slip, bank may call you to either correct the details or if it is not possible to do, we may ask you to take back your money. Crores of such rupees are deposited in Sundry Accounts of banks which are never credited to the correct accounts, since wrong details were given at the time of deposit and the one who deposited it have just forgotten about it.

I took the first deposit slip and it was a small deposit of 2000 Rs with mixed notes of 100/- and 500/-. I entered the account number in the system and checked the name which was exactly the same on the slip. Then I counted the note description with 5 notes of Rs 100 and 3 notes of Rs 500 and it tallied exactly. Now the deposit slip is in two parts, one the bigger portion is for bank in which all the details are given and which acts as a voucher for bank to keep it in records while the other counterpart which is smaller in size is for customer to have it as a receipt that he has deposited money.

I sat at the cash deposit counter and it was a different experience altogether. There was time when I had so much money in my counter that I had never ever seen in my life before. But it was public money and I was just a custodian of the same. I liked sitting with money all around me and I think nobody will hate to get a chance to spend whole day with bulk of currency notes even if it's not yours.

4 Hours had passed as it was almost lunch time, and my counter was empty.

"Sharma ji get your counter tallied with system and hand it over to me after lunch since there will be bulk deposit which you may have trouble counting. In addition to that, several applications and account openings forms are pending and Deovanshi sir need you there."

Saraiya sir asked me.

I started counting the money I had received and prepared packets of notes. I was not very good at it initially but Saraiya sir taught me the basics to arrange the notes with Gandhi Ji's photo on the same side in each note and always put the rubber band on the opposite side of Bapu.

I had received 22,34,500/- (Twenty-two lacs thirty-four thousand five hundred rupees) and was extremely happy to find the same number in the system. So, my physical cash and calculation was exactly the same with system and I handed it over to Saraiya sir with a smile since I had learnt another lesson in my banking life today.

My First Salary

Today was the tenth day since I joined Barhi branch and I was eagerly waiting for this day to come ever since I joined the bank. I still remember, I woke up before 7 in the morning and checked my mobile and there was an SMS from the bank regarding credit in bank account. Rs 14016/- were credited to my account and this was the biggest single credit in my account ever. I was so happy as finally the hard work had paid well. It was early in the morning and I was extremely happy. There are times when you are delighted from inside and it reflects from your body language. It was the month of January and the cold was at its peak and yet I took an early shower and got ready. I am the kind of person who rarely visits temples for worship or at least I never go alone. I have always followed my father's footstep and believed that God is within us and everywhere. Thus, praying to him does not require me to go somewhere particular. I prayed in my heart and thanked God for this life and the first person I really wanted to inform about it was my mother. Her sacrifices to make me what I am today are unmatchable.

"Mummy Salary aa gyi 14000 aayi hai."

I called my mother and informed.

"Bhagwan ka lakh lakh shukr hai. Bhagwan ko dhanyawad bolo aur tarakki den bhagwan tumhe."

She was happy and emotional at the same time. I could feel the heaviness in her voice.

"Nashta kiye beta kuchh?"

"Han mummy chane kha lia tha ab chai piunga bahar jakar."

My habit of eating sprouts was since hostel days. It's not only cheap but also very healthy vegetarian protein diet which does not require any cooking either.

If it was anyone else other than my mother, he/she may have expected something for them from my first salary, but the heart of the mother only cares about the child and despite knowing about my salary, she wanted to know whether I had eaten or not. The unconditional love of the mother is something one can never find anywhere else in the whole universe.

With such happy mood I called Rasika,

"Hi jaan! Good Morning."

"Good Morning Babu."

Till now she had developed this habit of sleeping in the train. Her group of 5 girls had this routine to get seats in sleeper class and they used to sleep because they had to get up early to catch the train from Jabalpur to Goteganw.

“Salary is credited have you seen?”

I asked in excitement.

“Yes 14016/- na I saw the message this morning. The best feeling ever.”

She replied in sleepy tone.

“Okay babu your voice is not clear maybe there is network issue here so I will call you later.”

“Okay jaan bye I love you.”

And we hang up. I got ready and left for office with a big smile.

Section 11

Quite some time had passed, and I started to enjoy working in a public sector bank but one thing that I missed was my friends. I never had a very big circle of friends ever but had a few of them in Katni and Jabalpur that I enjoyed spending time with. Here in Barhi I had colleagues in branch who were neither of my age nor were my kind of. Yes, Saraiya ji was a kind-hearted person but he was almost of the age of my father and Meena sir never really connected with me as a friend. Others rarely talk over topics other than banking.

It was Monday morning and I was just entering the branch in the morning when a young guy wearing specs asked me

"This is Barhi branch, right?"

"Yes, it is, and you are?" I asked

"I am Punit. Just reporting today."

He extended his hand for a handshake and I smiled at him. Finally, someone of my age was going to work in this branch.

"So, when did you complete your training bro?"

I asked him while giving a tour of the branch.

"Just last Saturday and today I am here."

He replied calmly.

I introduced Punit to the branch manager and they did exactly the same that was done during my initial days in the branch. I was happy because of two reasons. First reason of my happiness was that someone from my age group was joining the branch and the second reason was that before him, I was the junior most employee except sub staff, but from now on I will have someone who has joined the bank after me.

I was now settled in my job and had also made some friends in Barhi. As I sit here recounting the events of one weekend in Bandhavgarh, my heart still races with fear and relief. It all started with a simple plan: a weekend getaway with friends to the tiger reserve, a place of wild beauty and danger. Little did I know that our innocent excursion would turn into a nightmare of accusations and panic especially for me.

The journey to Bandhavgarh was filled with excitement. My friends and I rode our bikes through winding roads, surrounded by lush greenery. The thrill of adventure tingled in the air as we approached the forest. Barhi is at the border of Bandhavgarh and therefore, it does not take much time to reach to the core area of the tiger reserve. We parked our bikes and ventured deeper into the wilderness, ready to enjoy a day of relaxation and fun.

Setting up camp in a secluded spot, we cracked open beers and indulged in snacks, the laughter of friendship echoing through the trees. But during the discussion and roaming around the forest and river, we stumbled upon something that sent chills down our spines: the unmistakable marks of a tiger's feet imprinted in the earth. It was both thrilling and terrifying to realize that we were sharing the forest with such a magnificent predator.

"Sher kahin se bhi aa sakta hai bhai."

Punit said in a fearful tone.

"Indeed bro. Beer can get us killed."

I responded realizing the seriousness of the situation.

As the day wore on and the sun dipped below the horizon, we decided to call it a night. But sleep did not come easily as the thought of the tiger lingered in our minds. What if it decided to pay us a visit while we slept? The darkness seemed to stretch endlessly around us, alive with the sounds of the jungle.

The next day early morning, we reluctantly left the the forest behind and returned to the hustle and bustle of daily banking life. But my sense of unease only grew when I picked up the newspaper in office during the less crowdy hours and read the headline: "Tiger Killed in Bandhavgarh Reserve." Dread coiled in my stomach as I realized the implications of our presence in the forest the day before.

"Thank God brother we left the forest in time and nobody saw us. This could have dragged us in big trouble."

Punit said in troubled tone.

Panic set in when I reached for my wallet and found it missing. My ID card, the key to my identity, was nowhere to be found. Frantically searching through my belongings, I racked my brain trying to recall where I might have left it. And then it hit me like a ton of bricks – I must have dropped it in the forest during our partying. Yes, I carried my wallet there and had brought out the ID card while looking for cash.

The fear of being implicated in the tiger's death gripped me like a vice. In India, killing a tiger is not just a crime, it's a grave offense that carries severe consequences. My mind raced with worst-case scenarios as I imagined myself being dragged away by authorities, accused of a crime I didn't commit. I did not tell Punit or anyone else about my missing ID, but this was killing me from inside. I knew nobody will help me in this case as they will not want to be dragged into any sort of enquiry. I was even advised not to tell about our trip to forest to anybody especially in bank.

With trembling hands and a racing heart, I made a decision that would either save me or seal my fate. That night, under the cloak of darkness, I returned to the forest alone. It was a very tough decision and was a dangerous one since there are several other tigers in that region and they are mostly active at night. Every rustle of leaves and snap of twigs sent shivers down my spine as I retraced our steps from the previous day.

Hours passed in, trying to find my lost identity card, my desperation growing with each passing minute. I was going through the same path which we had chosen yesterday and where we had set up our camp. I remembered that we were also roaming around a nearby river where we had found the footmark of a tiger.

I had spent hours searching for my ID and was now losing patience. And then, just when I was on the verge of giving up hope, I spotted it – my ID card, lying half-submerged in the murky waters of the river.

Relief flooded through me like a tidal wave as I retrieved my card, clutching it to my chest as though it were a lifeline. With renewed determination, I made my way back to Barhi, the weight of fear and suspicion lifted from my shoulders.

Looking back on that harrowing experience, I am filled with gratitude for the stroke of luck that led me to find my ID card. But I am also haunted by the knowledge that, in the unforgiving wilderness of Bandhavgarh, a single misstep could have changed the course of my life forever.

Killing of an animal/pet is illegal and it is an offence being to cruelty on animals as defined under Section 11 of The Prevention Of Cruelty to Animals Act. It is a cognizable offence under Section 428 and Section 429 of the Indian Penal Code.

Late Night Calls

"I miss you too. But hey, let's talk about something lighter. Okay, tell me something, which is the most embarrassing moment of your life?" During one of the late-night phone calls I changed our topic of discussion which was getting serious.

"What? Embarrasing? I don't remember anything as of now Mayank. Wait a minute have I not done anything embarrassing in my life ever?"

She was confused.

"Okay, what about you? Which is the most embarrassing moment of your life?" She questioned me.

"I have gone through several embarrassing moments in my life such has been my experience but let me tell you about the one which I will never forget about."

"If I'm not wrong, I was at the age of 13 when this incident happened. We were at one of my relatives' houses. We all had gathered for the marriage function of one of my aunts. Those were the days when I was not accustomed with computers. Neither did we have computers in our home, nor did our school provided computer education. So, everyone, including my grandmother, mother, and and all other relatives were sitting inside this huge drawing room, which was having a computer. Son of my uncle named Akshay was playing a game in computer and I was just watching it sitting behind him. I was listening to the conversation of my relatives as well."

Rasika was listening carefully so I continued,

"Suddenly something weird happened and before going further into the details, let me tell you something. Those were the days when videos or other downloads were not available through Internet. It was really difficult to get the videos downloaded to mobile phones. Nokia was the leading mobile company those days and there was no Apple or Samsung, so to download a video into the mobile, computers or laptops were used. Father of Akshay, my uncle, used to download it into the mobile phones of others as it was one way of generating income. Therefore, he was having a huge collection of latest music videos, movies and also porn videos in his computer. Even though Akshay was having a little bit of computer literacy, but he was no expert and was not aware of all the functions and controls."

"A speaker was also connected to the computer; therefore, the sound was also on the higher side. So out of nowhere suddenly a full hard-core gang bang porn video started playing on the screen of computer. I do not know neither did Akshay what he actually did, but it started playing. Everyone including me in the room were shocked and embarrassed because of the shameful situation we were in. Akshay was too little to understand what was happening. I could not dare to look behind and see the expressions of my other relatives, including my mother and grandmother. I wanted to hide myself somewhere even if I was not the cause of the chaos, yet I found it very embarrassing, more importantly, I did not know how to turn that off. Actually no one in in that room knew how to turn it off. So, it kept playing for some while and the sounds were getting louder and louder. I do not want to go into the details about what was actually happening in that video but you can imagine."

"What"

Rasika was shocked and started laughing so hard.

"Wait na listen to me Rasika, please let me complete."

I narrated further,

"Suddenly an idea came in my mind, let it be a computer about which I knew nothing, but all appliances need power. So, I stood up and pulled the power plug out of the socket and as soon as the computer was turned off, I ran out. Everyone was shouting at Akshay and his mother started beating him. This incident was the most embarrassing one and nobody talked about it ever again."

"What? Really that is shocking Mayank, but I can imagine how you must be feeling."

Laughter and nostalgia filled the air as we recounted the misadventure of mine.

As the conversation flowed, we seamlessly transitioned from laughter to more profound discussions. Dreams, fears, and the intricacies of our lives spilled into the night airwaves. I spoke about my aspirations and the quiet satisfaction I found in the chaos of Barhi.

Rasika, in turn, shared the challenges of balancing work and personal life in Gotegaon, the pressures she faced, the not so tasty food and the dreams she held close to her heart. In those late-night conversations, the miles between us seemed to dissolve, and our heartbeat in harmony through the digital connection.

As the night deepened, I asked, "Do you ever wonder how different our lives would be if we had never met in SBTC?"

Rasika's thoughtful silence lingered before she responded, "It's a scary thought, isn't it? I can't imagine my life without you now. You've become such an integral part of it."

I nodded in agreement, though Rasika couldn't see me, "Sometimes, I think about the randomness of it all. How a single decision or a chance encounter could have changed everything. But I'm grateful for every twist and turn that led me to you."

Our conversation shifted to quieter tones, the weight of unspoken emotions filling the virtual space between us. We shared our vulnerabilities, expressing the fears that lingered beneath the surface of our love.

"But I've been thinking about something, and I wanted to talk to you about it Rasika." I exclaimed.

Rasika's curiosity piqued. "What is it?"

I took a deep breath, gathering my thoughts. "I was thinking about us—about our love story," I began. "And I had this idea..."

I could hear the excitement in Rasika's voice as she urged me to continue. "What idea?"

"Well," I said hesitantly, "I was thinking about writing a novel about us. About our journey together, the ups and downs, the laughter and tears. I want to capture our love story in words, immortalize it on paper."

There was a pause on the other end of the line, and for a moment, I feared I had said too much. But then Rasika spoke, her voice filled with emotion. "That's... that's beautiful," she whispered. "I would love to read a novel about us, about our love."

Her words filled me with a sense of purpose and determination. "I want to do it justice," I said earnestly. "I want to pour my heart and soul into this novel, to make it a tribute to our love."

Rasika's laughter echoed through the phone, a sound that warmed my heart. "I have no doubt you'll do just that," she said softly. "You have a gift for storytelling, and our love story is one worth telling."

We talked late into the night, brainstorming ideas and reminiscing about our journey together. With each word spoken, I felt a renewed sense of inspiration and passion. This novel wasn't just a project—it was a labor of love, a testament to the bond we shared.

As the night wore on, I yawned, my exhaustion catching up with me. "I guess it's time for me to call it a night, beautiful. Another day closer to being together."

Rasika's voice softened, "Sleep well, Mayank. Dream of our future together."

I whispered my goodnight, disconnecting the call but carrying the echoes of Rasika's voice into my dreams. In those quiet moments, as the city outside slept, I found solace in the knowledge that love could transcend the boundaries of time and space, and our shared journey continued through the night and beyond.

As we said our goodbyes and hung up the phone, I felt a sense of excitement and anticipation building within me. This novel would be my love letter to Rasika, a tribute to the woman who had captured my heart and changed my life forever.

"Chapter -I SBTC" were the first few words as I sat down and started to write. Words flowed effortlessly from my fingertips, each sentence a testament to the love that had brought us together and would continue to guide us on our journey ahead.

A Surprise Stopover

Despite the geographical distance, my connection with Rasika grew stronger with each passing day, fuelled by late-night calls and heartfelt messages.

My work often demanded late hours, yet I eagerly awaited our nightly conversations. The hum of Barhi outside my room's terrace seemed to fade away as I focused on Rasika's laughter and the stories she shared about her day. The digital connection bridged the physical miles between us.

One fateful weekend, I decided it was time to surprise Rasika. I secretly booked a train to Gotegaon, envisioning the joy that would light up her face when I appeared at her doorstep. As I stepped off the train, excitement and nerves mingled within me, creating a whirlwind of emotions.

Rasika had started to live with her friends in Gotegaon since daily up down was becoming a tiresome task and during weekends they had this practice of going to Jabalpur to visit their home. Rasika had earlier informed me that she was not going to Jabalpur this weekend as she had too many clothes to wash and will also be alone since other girls had no plans of staying. Realizing this was a great opportunity I had planned this trip.

Arriving at Rasika's apartment, my heart raced. Suddenly an idea came in my mind and I called her standing just outside her room.

"Good morning jaan."

"Hey, a very good morning to you babu."

She was still sleepy.

"What are you doing Rasika?"

I asked her knowing it's a holiday and she must still be sleeping.

"Still in bed babu what about you?"

She asked in her usual sleepy tone.

"Standing outside your room."

I said playfully.

"Oh, I really wish you were here Mayank. Nobody is here. Remember how you always wanted to come in my room in SBTC."

She was remembering our awesome time in SBTC.

"Open the door na."

I tried to sound serious.

"Don't play with me Mayank."

She did not believe me.

"For me please once open the door na babe."

I tried to convince her.

Gotegaon, where Rasika was living and posted, was a small town and people in such cities are very judgemental when it comes to a young guy and girl meeting alone. I knew this fact because I was from one such city and with all the nervousness, I pressed the bell.

The door swung open, revealing Rasika's surprised expression, followed by a burst of laughter and tears of joy.

"Whattt? What are you doing here Mayank?"

She was so surprised to see me.

"Tumne bulaya aur ham chale aaye."

I replied singing this for her.

We hugged tightly standing at the door itself which was quite odd for people living in nearby rooms. It was a huge building where other tenants were also living. Realizing the weird look on the faces of her neighbours, she pulled me inside the room and shut the door.

"Are you crazy?" How did you know I was alone?"

She asked me in excitement.

"You only told me Rasika."

I was looking in her eyes and was continuously smiling. It was the moment I was waiting from quite some time. Ever since we left SBTC, this was the first time that we were meeting alone like this.

The weekend unfolded as a beautiful blend of exploring Gotegaon together and cherishing the simple moments.

Though Gotegaon was a small town and there wasn't much to explore yet we were happy just because we were together.

I brought her chocolate which I had bought from Gotegaon only and yes Roses as she loved them. She was extremely happy to have me with her. I helped her with the household, and we spent the whole day together. I made Maggie and Tea for her which she loved the most. We spent the day mostly in bed doing what we loved the most and yes, we also talked a lot.

Reality hit as Sunday evening approached, and I had to catch my return train to Barhi. The temporary togetherness had intensified our longing, making it even more challenging to part ways.

She came to Railway station to drop me.

"I can't believe how two days have passed and you are already going."

She was crying.

"Seriously Rasika. It feels like I had just arrived and now I am going back."

I replied sadly to her.

The railway station goodbyes were bittersweet, but the shared memories fuelled our determination to navigate the challenges posed by distance.

As days passed, I and Rasika discovered the strength of our connection. We navigated the work pressures and the occasional bouts of loneliness. Virtual dates became our refuge, allowing us to share meals, watch movies together, and celebrate milestones despite being miles apart.

Night Encounter with Tiger

After that incident of losing my ID card near Abandhavgarh where a tiger was killed, we never visited bandhavgarh again. One unforgettable night we left behind the previous horrific memory and set out with a local driver into the jungle, seeking the elusive beauty of the wild. It was all around the news that a tigress in Bandhavgarh has given birth to three beautiful cubs and tourists were reaching in big numbers to witness that.

As the sun dipped below the horizon, I along with Punit and other staff of our branch eagerly gathered for our night adventure. The anticipation in the air was palpable, fuelled by the stories of tigers that roamed freely in the dense forest just beyond the village of Barhi.

Our local driver Mohan, well-versed in navigating the pathways of the jungle, added an element of reassurance to the adventure. The chatter in the vehicle grew animated as we left the village behind.

"Imagine witnessing a tigress with her cubs in the wild," I exclaimed, as my eyes alight with enthusiasm. "It's a rare spectacle, and we would be incredibly fortunate if have such opportunity."

"Sorry sir but I doubt that you are going to see any tigers tonight." Said Mohan in a serious tone.

"Why Mohan bhaiya?" We all almost shouted together in a shock.

"Two tigers are never seen together at one place. One is already here so..." Mohan indirectly called himself a tiger and we all laughed at his brilliant joke.

Mohan, who had grown up in the shadows of the Bandhavgarh forest, shared his experiences of multiple encounters with the majestic tigers, adding a layer of authenticity to the unfolding adventure.

As we went deeper into the forest, the atmosphere within the vehicle became charged with anticipation. Suddenly, the crackling of dry leaves under the tires ceased, and Mohan signalled us for silence. The air was pregnant with expectation as we strained our ears to catch any sound of the tigers. In the stillness of the night, the jungle seemed to hold its breath, creating an otherworldly ambiance.

Then, as if nature itself granted us a moment of serendipity, a tigress emerged from the shadows. Her majestic form, bathed in moonlight, exuded a regal aura. Beside her walked three playful cubs, they were so adorable contrasting with the fierce elegance of their mother. Silently sitting in the vehicle, we collectively held our breath, awe-struck by the rare spectacle unfolding before us.

My voice barely above a whisper, marvelled at the scene. "This is once-in-a-lifetime experience. Look at the grace and beauty of these creatures."

The tigress and her cubs moved with an effortless grace. The headlights cast an ephemeral glow on their sleek fur, creating a scene that would forever be captured in our memories.

Mohan provided detailed commentary on the behavior of the tigers. His knowledge added depth to our appreciation of the scene, turning a casual wildlife sighting into an educational and awe-inspiring encounter.

As the minutes ticked by, the tigress led her cubs deeper into the wilderness, gradually disappearing from view. Still caught in the magic of the moment, we found our voices returning.

"I can't believe we just witnessed that," Punit exclaimed, his eyes wide with amazement.

I replied, "Nature has a way of leaving us in awe. This experience is a testament to the beauty and wildness that exists just beyond our everyday lives."

Our trip was successful as we had witnessed tigress along with her three cubs. People spend thousands of rupees in Tiger Reserve just to see a glimpse of tigers and here we were so fortunate that we witnessed it without paying anything to anybody.

The journey back to the village was accompanied by a symphony of laughter, animated conversations, and shared reflections on the encounter. Bound by the experience of witnessing the tigress and her cubs, we felt a profound connection to the untamed world that coexisted with our everyday lives.

As we approached Barhi, the headlights of the vehicle pierced through the darkness, revealing the familiar landscape that now seemed touched by the mystical aura of the jungle. We were changed forever by our night in the wild, carried with us not just memories of a tigress and her cubs but a newfound appreciation for the delicate balance between civilization and the untamed wilderness.

The Bank PO Interview

During the year 2012, I had appeared in a number of competitive exams along with SBB clerk exam and one of them was Bank Probationary Officer exam. Recently the result of the written exam was declared and both I and Rasika had cleared it. Now the next step was interview for the same.

In the heart of Jabalpur, where the Narmada River weaves its way through the city, I found myself at a crucial juncture in my professional journey. In formal attire armed with a wealth of banking knowledge, I stepped into the interview room for the IBPS PO exam. Nervous yet determined, my interview in Jabalpur turned out to be a mixed bag of emotions.

As I sat in the waiting area, anticipation and nervous energy filled the room. The atmosphere was charged with a mix of excitement and apprehension as candidates from various backgrounds and experiences prepared to face the interview panel. For me, who had diligently prepared for the PO exam, this moment marked the culmination of months of hard work and dedication.

The interview room in Jabalpur, with its official decor and a panel of seasoned bankers, seemed to amplify the significance of the occasion. With a resume that spoke of my experience in a rural branch, I knew that the questions could vary from banking procedures to my ability to adapt to different environments.

"Mr. Mayank Sharma."

As my name was called into the interview room, I couldn't help but feel a surge of nervousness. The panel, with their keen eyes and poised demeanour, greeted me. The questions began, probing into my educational background, work experience, and understanding of the banking sector.

Interviewer: Good morning! Please have a seat. So, you're here for the bank officer position. Can you tell me a little about yourself Mayank?

Mayank: Good morning sir! I am a B. Com graduate and currently working with Swift Bank of Bharat as an SWO-1.

Interviewer: Let's talk about your experience. What relevant skills and experience do you bring to this role?

Mayank: Well, I've worked in customer service sir, so I know how to handle all sorts of characters – from the grumpy ones to the overly enthusiastic ones. I'm also good at multitasking.

Interviewer: Now, let's say you encounter a difficult customer who's upset about an issue with their account. How would you handle it?

Mayank: Well, first, I'd listen carefully to their concerns because sometimes people just need to vent. Then, I'd apologize for the inconvenience and assure them that I'll do everything in my power to resolve the issue.

Interviewer: Where do you see yourself in five years?

Mayank: Honestly, I see myself growing and excelling in this role. Maybe I'll even become the CEO of the bank one day – stranger things have happened, right?

The turning point in the interview came when I was asked about my experience working in a rural branch near Bandhavgarh. The panel, recognizing the uniqueness of my posting, sought to test not only my banking knowledge but also the adaptability and knowledge of the local context.

"Mayank, can you share some insights into the challenges and opportunities you faced while working in a rural branch in Barhi?" inquired one of the panel members.

Though initially nervous, I drew a deep breath and began to narrate my experiences. I spoke about the challenges of catering to the financial needs of a predominantly agrarian community. I also highlighted the importance of financial inclusion in such areas and the satisfaction I derived from being a part of the community's growth.

The panel, impressed by my sincerity and depth of understanding, nodded in acknowledgment. The conversation then took an unexpected turn when one of the interviewers asked, "Bandhavgarh was in news today can you tell us what it was about?"

Ever since I started preparing for government job examinations, everyone from teachers to seniors emphasised on reading newspaper everyday. Today while I was travelling from Barhi to Jabalpur, I had purchased 'Dainik Bhaskar' in train and there was this news of the three cubs who were recently born in Bandhavgarh. With my brightening face, I seized the opportunity to showcase my knowledge beyond banking. With a genuine smile, I spoke about them and the panel was impressed.

As the interview progressed, the questions shifted back to banking, covering topics ranging from financial regulations to customer relations.

Having navigated the interview with a mix of humility and expertise, I felt a sense of accomplishment. This interview had not only tested my banking knowledge but had allowed me to showcase the versatility and adaptability.

Interviewer: Noted! Have a great day!

Mayank: Good day sir! Take care!

As the interview concluded, the panel commended me for comprehensive responses and the unique blend of skills that I brought to the table. Walking out of the interview room, I couldn't help but reflect on the unexpected joy that discussing Bandhavgarh had brought me during the nerve-wracking experience.

The news of my success in the IBPS PO exam reached a few weeks later when my name was in the list of successful candidates who cleared the interview as well, filling me with a profound sense of achievement. The mixed emotions which I experienced during the interview in Jabalpur, from nervousness to pride, now became part of a success story that would shape my future in the banking sector.

Chapter V

Doubt and Dilemma

It was March 2013 and four months had passed since I joined Swift Bank of Bharat. In the glow of our recent successes, I and Rasika found ourselves at a pivotal crossroads in our professional lives. Both of us had successfully cleared the interview for probationary officer positions in two distinguished banks – I was to join in Unite Bank of India and Rasika in Crystal Bank. As we navigated the possibilities of our futures, a long phone call ensued, where Rasika, confident about her decision to leave the Swift Bank of Bharat, sought to convince me to embrace change and explore the opportunities that awaited us.

The crackling warmth of the phone call resonated through the airwaves as I and Rasika settled into a conversation that would shape the trajectory of our careers.

"Mayank, I've been thinking a lot about this, and I'm convinced that stepping out of our comfort zones is essential for personal and professional growth. Crystal Bank offers a unique set of challenges and learning opportunities, and I believe it's the right move for me. What about you?" Rasika inquired, her voice a blend of anticipation and determination.

I, on the other end of the line, hesitated for a moment. The security of my current position in the Swift Bank of Bharat and the familiarity of my routine whispered caution in ears. "Rasika, you know how things are at the Swift Bank. It's stable, and I'm comfortable. Unite Bank of India is a great opportunity, no doubt, but there's a sense of attachment here."

Rasika, recognizing the weight of my words, responded with empathy. "I understand, Mayank. Change is scary and leaving behind what's familiar is never easy. But consider the potential for growth, exposure to new challenges, and the chance to diversify your skills. We've worked hard to get here, and this could be the leap we need to elevate our careers."

Rasika, undeterred by the uncertainty, painted vivid pictures of the exciting challenges that awaited us in our new roles.

"Think about it, Mayank. Unite Bank of India could offer you a platform to expand your skill set, work with a diverse set of colleagues, and broaden your horizons. It's not about leaving behind what's comfortable; it's about embracing the potential for growth and self-discovery."

Torn between the familiarity of the Swift Bank and the allure of a new opportunity, I acknowledged Rasika's perspective. "I get what you're saying, Rasika. It's just that I've grown attached to the team, the routine, and the work culture here. Leaving all that behind feels like a significant step into the unknown."

Rasika, her voice gentle yet resolute, replied, "Change is uncomfortable, Mayank, but it's important for progress. We can't let fear of the unknown hold us back from seizing new opportunities. The fact that we're having this conversation means we're ready for the next chapter in our careers."

As the conversation unfolded, Rasika began to share her own considerations and the factors that had led her to embrace the change. She spoke of the potential for networking, the exposure to different banking practices, and the thrill of stepping into a dynamic work environment.

"Mayank, we've both worked hard to secure this opportunity. I believe that leaving the Swift Bank, as emotionally challenging as it may be, is the right move for both of us."

I was feeling a mixture of emotions, reflected on Rasika's words. The idea of starting a new journey, although daunting, began to resonate with me. Rasika, sensing the shift in my perspective, continued to reinforce the idea that change, though intimidating, was an integral part of growth.

"Mayank, remember the satisfaction we felt when we received the news about clearing the interviews? That excitement, that anticipation of something new – that's the energy we need to channel now. Unite Bank of India could be the canvas for new achievements and experiences for you."

The conversation turned toward the support we could provide to each other during this transition.

"Mayank, we're not alone in this. We have each other, and we have the skills and knowledge we've gained so far. This isn't just a job change; it's a step towards realizing our aspirations. Let's embrace it together and turn this uncertainty into an adventure."

As the call neared its end, I found myself leaning towards the prospect of change.

"Rasika, you've given me a lot to think about. Change is indeed scary, but you're right – it's also exciting. Let's embrace this together and make the most of the opportunities that come our way. Unite Bank of India sounds like an adventure waiting to happen."

The airwaves carried a sense of resolution as we, with a shared commitment to growth and new experiences, concluded our conversation. The decision to leave the Swift Bank of Bharat was still marked by uncertainty, but the seeds of anticipation had been sown, and a new chapter awaited us in the halls of Unite Bank of India and Crystal Bank. Bound by shared aspirations and a commitment to each other, we set forth to navigate the uncharted waters of our evolving careers.

The Resignation

In the corridors of the Swift Bank of Bharat, where I had spent a significant portion of my professional journey, an important decision was brewing. After long discussions with friends, family, and colleagues, I had made up my mind. I was about to bid farewell to the familiar routine, the known faces, and the comforting rhythm of my current job. The reason behind this change? A new opportunity awaited me at Unite Bank of India, a prospect that promised growth, challenge, and a fresh chapter in my career.

The decision to resign from a stable and well-established position in Swift Bank of Bharat was not made lightly.

Meticulous and thoughtful in my approach, I sought counsel from those who mattered most to me.

First on the list were my friends, the trusted confidants with whom I had shared not just professional experiences but also the personal issues of life.

My friend, Ankush, who had joined the bank with me and had strategic thinking, was the first to respond. "Mayank, you've got to compare the pros and cons. Leaving the Swift Bank is undoubtedly a big step, but if Unite Bank is offering you a platform for growth and a chance to broaden your horizons, it's worth considering."

Ankush had also cleared the interview and he was going to Join Overseas bank.

Other than Ankush, I also talked with several other friends. Some of them emphasized the importance of embracing change, while others pointed out the potential for learning and advancement in a new environment. The collective opinion of my friends became a valuable compass guiding me towards a decision that aligned with my aspirations.

Encouraged by the support of my friends, I turned to my family for guidance.

My father spoke first. "Beta, life is a journey of exploration and growth. If this opportunity at Unite Bank aligns with your goals and ambitions, don't let the fear of leaving the familiar hold you back. We believe in your abilities, and we'll support your decision wholeheartedly."

My mother added, "Change is always accompanied by a mix of emotions, but it's in those moments of discomfort that we often find our true potential. You have our blessings, Mayank."

I took the next step – discussing the decision with my colleagues at the Swift Bank of Bharat. The news, initially met with surprise, opened the floodgates to a series of conversations.

As the discussions unfolded, credit officer of our branch, who had gone through similar transitions in the past, offered a piece of advice. "Mayank, change is like a double-edged sword – it brings both challenges and opportunities. But growth often lies in the uncomfortable spaces outside our comfort zones. If Unite Bank offers you a chance to grow, consider it seriously."

Having insights from my friends, family, and the valuable counsel of colleagues, I found clarity in the midst of the decision-making process. The prospect of joining Unite Bank of India began to shimmer with promise, and the fear of leaving behind the familiar began to transform into a sense of anticipation.

With my decision solidified, I embarked on the daunting yet liberating journey of resigning from the Swift Bank of Bharat. The official letter, written with a mix of gratitude and a forward-looking spirit, was submitted to my branch manager who further forwarded it to RBO Katni. The pretty HR manager who once had handed me the joining letter, called me numerous times to rethink about my decision of resigning from the Swift Bank of Bharat.

Shruti: Hello Mayank, this is Shruti from HR. I heard you're resigning from the bank. Can we talk about it?

Mayank: Hi ma'm. Yeah, I've made up my mind. I appreciate the opportunity here, but I think it's time for a change as I have cleared PO interview and will be joining as an Officer there.

Shruti: I understand, Mayank. But before you make your final decision, can we discuss what's making you want to leave as you can be promoted as an Officer here as well and SBB is a bigger bank?

Mayank: Well, it's not anything personal against the bank. I just feel like I need a new challenge, you know. Something different and promotion here will take time and as both are government banks, I do not think it will make any difference.

Shruti: I get it, change can be refreshing. But have you considered all the opportunities for growth and advancement within our organization?

Mayank: I have, and I really appreciate the career development opportunities here. It's just that I had given PO exam along with SBB and result is declared now. It will take another three to five years in SBB to become an officer while here I am directly going to join as an officer in Unite Bank of India.

Shruti: I see. Well, Mayank, we value your contributions to the bank, and we'd hate to see you go. Is there anything we can do to make you reconsider?

Mayank: I appreciate your concern, Ma'm. But I've thought about it a lot, and I think it's best for me to move on. Thank you for understanding.

Shruti: Of course, Mayank. We'll miss you around here. If you ever change your mind or need anything, don't hesitate to reach out.

Mayank: Thanks, ma'm. I'll keep that in mind. Take care.

An employee is an asset to any institute and HR team tried hard not to let me go easily.

After my resignation was accepted, I was given two options, either to serve the notice period of 15 days or deposit a demand draft equal to the amount of my 15 days salary. I chose the latter options since I did not want to delay joining Unite Bank of India as I was guided by the seniors that earlier you join, better are the chances of getting a good branch posting.

The farewell, a bittersweet moment that marked the end of an era, was marked by warm wishes and promises to stay in touch. My colleagues, recognizing the significance of my decision, expressed admiration for my courage to embrace change. I still remember what my branch manager Mr. Babulal Labade told me on my last day,

"Mud kar mat dekhna Sharma." And I never looked back.

The final day at the Swift Bank of Bharat unfolded with a series of heartfelt goodbyes. Surrounded by colleagues who had been part of my journey, I felt a sense of nostalgia and gratitude. The familiar faces, the routines, and friendship were etched in my memory as I stepped out of the office for the last time.

As I walked away from the known towards the unknown, I couldn't help but reflect on the transformative power of change. The decision to resign from the Swift Bank, made me sad, but It was overshadowed by the anticipation of new beginnings. Unite Bank of India awaited me with its promise of fresh challenges, diverse experiences, and the potential for professional growth.

Chapter VI

Fresh Horizon

It was April 2013 and I left for Bhopal taking a train from Katni and Rasika joined me in the same train to Bhopal as she caught it from Jabalpur. The air was thick with a blend of emotions – excitement, nervousness, and a tinge of sadness as I left behind the familiar landscapes of my past. Zonal office of Unite Bank of India was situated in Bhopal and I was to report there. Rasika accompanied me on this transformative adventure and a new chapter of my life. While checking into a hotel in Bhopal, we found ourselves caught between the anticipation of what lay ahead and the bittersweet reflection on the life we were leaving behind.

I couldn't help but feel a sense of nostalgia for the life I was leaving behind in my hometown. Rasika, attuned to my feelings, offered a comforting presence as we settled into the room where we were going to stay for the next couple of days.

"Mayank, its okay to feel a bit emotional. This is a big step, and it's only natural to reflect on what we're leaving behind," Rasika remarked, her eyes reflecting understanding and empathy.

Grateful for her insight, I nodded in agreement. "You're right, Rasika. It's just that leaving behind friends, family, and the familiar faces at Swift Bank is harder than I thought."

Rasika took my hand in hers. "Change is never easy, but it's a part of life. This new journey is not just about a new job; it's about growth, new experiences, and the adventure of building a future together."

As we unpacked our belongings, my thoughts wandered between the memories I was leaving behind and the possibilities that awaited me at Unite Bank. Rasika decided to steer the conversation towards the positive aspects of the move.

"Mayank, think about the new friends we'll make, the experiences we'll share, and the memories we'll create in new places. Let's embrace this change together and make the most of it."

Her words acted as a gentle reminder, injecting a sense of optimism into the air. Determined to face this new beginning hand in hand, we decided to explore the city and make the most of our time together before I delved into the demands of my new job.

In the evening, as we returned to the hotel room, a sense of calm had settled over me. The emotional chaos had given way to a newfound excitement for the adventures that awaited us.

Against the backdrop of the city lights, we found ourselves immersed in a different kind of energy – the quiet romance that comes with shared dreams and aspirations. The hotel room, now bathed in a soft glow, created a romantic setup, a pause in our journey to savor the love that had brought us together.

Rasika, sensing the shift in my mood, decided to infuse the evening with a touch of romance. She dimmed the lights, and soft music filled the air as we sat by the window, the city lights twinkling in the distance.

"Mayank, this is our moment. A moment to celebrate not just the challenges we're facing but also the love that binds us together. Let's make this evening about us," Rasika suggested, her eyes reflecting the warmth of her sentiment.

The city outside, with its bustling life, faded into the background as we created a cocoon of togetherness within the confines of the hotel room. We made love that evening and I was now more relaxed and present in the moment.

Next day I reported to Zonal office of Unite Bank of India. It did not take me long since my order was already prepared and was handed me over as soon as I reached. I was given Nagri Niwas branch. The location was not known to me and I tried to Google it. With my limited geographical knowledge, I thought Niwas was somewhere near Indore, but my branch was not just 'Niwas' but 'Nagri Niwas'. Even after long research, I could not come to any conclusion, so I asked the officer sitting in front, "excuse me may I know under which Region does branch of Nagri Niwas comes."

I was informed that it comes under Rewa Region. I was not happy at all about this new posting as later I came to know that the exact location of the branch was in Singrauli district. Even when I was about to join Swift Bank of Bharat,

I was trying to avoid Sigrauli, but as they say God has his own plans for everyone.

Quandary of Quitting

Reaching and reporting Nagri Niwas branch was quite some task as there was no direct train from Bhopal. First, I went to Rewa district to report to the Regional office and then I was directed towards Nagri Niwas branch. Before leaving for Nagri Niwas, I tried so hard to get my posting order changed by Rewa Regional Office, but all my efforts were failed. The officials told me that I am quite lucky to get a branch posting which also has Railway route and the place is very scenic with mountains and waterfalls.

The route to my proposed branch was through a tiring bus journey. Firstly, I took a bus from Rewa to Sidhi district of Madhya Pradesh and then changed a bus from Sidhi and caught another bus to Nigri. Nigri or Nagri was the village where my branch was located, and it was exactly between the district of Sidhi and Singrauli. As I embarked on my journey to Nagri Niwas, I found myself on a bus traversing winding road that seemed to lead to the very edge of civilization. The anticipation of a new professional challenge mingled with the uncertainties of navigating life in one of the most remote villages in the country.

The bustling city life slowly gave way to open fields, quaint hamlets, and the rhythmic hum of the bus, which seemed to echo the heartbeat of the remote region I was entering into. As the bus moved further away from the comfort of urban amenities, my surroundings began to reflect the raw beauty of rural India.

The challenges that lay ahead loomed in my thoughts – a branch located in one of the most remote villages meant not just professional hurdles but a complete immersion into a lifestyle that vastly contrasted with the urban comfort I was accustomed to.

After a long journey of 7 hours as the bus rolled into Nagri Niwas, I was greeted by a landscape that felt both enchanting and daunting. Singrauli is known for coal and there were numerous coal power plants and mines.

Disembarking from the bus, I was met with curious glances from the locals. The sight of a banker arriving in their secluded village was an event that sparked both interest and speculation.

Google map location was of no use since there was only one road from which the bus had arrived and there was no sign of any branch around the point I was dropped. I was in Nigri Village and was unable to locate the branch where I was to report. I enquired from the locals and they informed me that the branch was located in Niwas village. All this while I was assuming Nagri and Niwas to be the same village, but both were different.

I came here with the initial plan of living for the next 15 days till I find shelter and therefore, I had this bag with me. While trying to get an idea about the route to my branch, I was unable to communicate well since locals spoke Bagheli language in that part of India. Bagheli is a kind of local Hindi language but was not even close to what I was used to speaking and understanding. I noticed they all were gazing at me like I was from some other planet.

I was very confused because nobody was able to guide me the correct route to the branch and it was already getting dark. Suddenly, I remembered that officials from Rewa Regional Office had given me contact details of the branch manager and accountant of the branch. First, I dialled the number of Branch manager and just after the two rings he picked up.

"Hello."

He said

"Hello. Sir I am Mayank Sharma the new officer. I have arrived here, but the bus dropped me at Nigri, and I am unable to locate the branch."

I informed him about my difficulties as I was now getting nervous in this strange village where I did not know anybody.

"Mayank Ji it is only 3 KM from Nigri village, and you just need to walk straight on the road you are standing."

Branch manager sounded like a drunk man in his early 40s.

I thought really? "There must be autos around because I have this trolly with me sir."

I conveyed him the difficulty I was going through.

"Mayank Ji you will not find any auto here since its already past 6:00." He replied.

I was travelling from last night when I caught the train from Bhopal to Rewa. Then I changed two buses and travelled whole day to reach here and I had not yet arrived at my destination.

"Okay sir."

I replied and having no other option started walking towards the direction I was guided by the branch manager sir. I was too tired but had to walk with the heavy trolly and a bag on my back. Soon I started sweating badly as the temperature is normally on the higher side in Singrauli and there was no proper road as well. It took me almost 20 minutes to walk on the dusty road when I finally reached Niwas Village and still, I was unable to locate the branch.

"Where is Unite Bank of India?"

I asked the Panwala bhaiya.

"Apna panche peechhe mudi babuji." ("Look behind sir.")

He replied and I saw a small old building was there just beside the canal which was dry as a desert. The only sign of this building being a bank was a tilted old board in which even the bulb was fused.

As I reached closer, I was greeted not by the familiar hum of air conditioning or the orderly queues of urban banking but by the vibrant chaos of rural life. The branch, housed within a modest structure, was filled with over a hundred villagers engaged in various activities and I was shocked to see this since branch timing is generally till 4 PM and here the whole premises was packed with customers even after 6 PM. Finding my way through the crowded space, I realized that the challenges of this new assignment were not limited to the professional domain.

The lack of air conditioning and proper ventilation immediately struck me as I entered the branch. The air inside hung heavy with the amalgamation of various scents – a mix of earth, sweat, and aroma of the nearby agricultural fields. The absence of modern amenities that I had taken for granted in Barhi branch served as a reminder that my role in Nagri Niwas was more than just banking; it was an immersion into a way of life that demanded adaptability.

The limited space within the branch echoed with the constant chatter of villagers, the clatter of transactions, and the occasional sounds of livestock from the nearby fields.

Navigating through the sea of villagers, I tried to find the cabin of branch manager, but to my surprise there was only one cabin inside the small building and it looked more like a prison and cash was being deposited and withdrawn from the same counter. The absence of the polished interiors and sophisticated technology that defined my previous workspace only fueled me with nervousness and doubt about my decision to leave SBB.

The noise level inside the branch was substantial, with villagers engaged in conversations, children playing in corners, and the occasional outbursts of laughter.

The absence of air conditioning, along with the warm, humid climate, intensified the natural scents of the rural surroundings.

Upon arrival, I encountered Mr. Happy Rai who was from Lucknow and looked so sweet and intelligent and Mr. Meena, who was retired from navy, hailing from Rajasthan. Branch manager was not there in the branch and later when I met him, he was drunk. Consuming alcohol during work hours was something I was not expecting at least from a branch manager.

As I nervously stepped into the branch manager's house where he had called me, I couldn't help but feel a knot forming in my stomach. It was my first day at the bank, and I was already greeted by an unexpected sight – the branch manager, slouched in a chair, appeared to be drunk.

"Um, excuse me, sir," I stammered, unsure of how to proceed. "I'm Mayank, the new officer. I was told to report to you."

The branch manager lifted his head slightly, looking at me through bleary eyes. "Ah, another one, huh? Sit down, Mayank," he slurred, gesturing towards a chair with a lazy wave of his hand.

I cautiously took a seat, trying to ignore the overwhelming smell of alcohol in the room. "Is everything okay, sir?" I asked, feeling a mixture of concern and discomfort.

"Okay? Ha!" he scoffed bitterly. "This place is a dump, Mayank. A godforsaken village in the middle of nowhere. No facilities, no amenities – just dust and despair."

I shifted uncomfortably in my seat, unsure of how to respond. This wasn't exactly the warm welcome I had been expecting on my first day. "I… I'm sorry to hear that, sir," I murmured awkwardly, not knowing what else to say.

The branch manager let out a heavy sigh, slumping further into his chair. "You'll see, Mayank. This place will suck the life out of you. No one cares about us here – not the higher-ups, not the government. We're just a forgotten outpost in the vast expanse of Singrauli."

I couldn't help but feel a wave of discouragement wash over me. Was this really what I had signed up for? A dead-end job in a neglected corner of the world? I had been hopeful and excited about starting my career at the Unite Bank, but now all I could see was the bleakness of my surroundings.

"I understand, sir," I said quietly, trying to keep the disappointment out of my voice. "But... but surely there must be some positives about working here, right? Some opportunities for growth and development?"

The branch manager let out a bitter laugh, shaking his head in resignation. "Oh, Mayank. You're young, ambitious – I can see it in your eyes. But trust me, there's no future for you here. This place will crush your spirit, just like it did mine."

I felt a sinking feeling in the pit of my stomach as I realized the magnitude of his words. Was I destined to become just another disillusioned soul, trapped in the suffocating grip of Singrauli's despair?

After spending good half an hour at his place, I chose to leave, and he did not stop me either. I went back to the branch which was still operating at 6:30 PM.

I somehow spent the first day in this branch and I literally felt like crying. I felt as if I was stuck in a prison and the place seemed like hell to me. As I had come with a bag having clothes for a fortnight, I was forced to spend next few days here. I somehow tried to convince myself to stay and not take any hasty decision. The branch was completely packed with customers till 6:30 PM and then it took another 2 hours for staff to complete the work and close the branch. Usually general public in cities have this idea that banks only operate till 4 PM but we must end the day in system, and we are allowed to close it only after clearing all the tasks.

When finally, at 8:30 PM we were ready to close the branch, I saw no sub staff was available and it was dark outside the branch. I turned on the flashlight of my mobile phone as Happy sir locked the premises.

"Where are the sub staff to lock the door sir?"

I asked in curiosity.

"He must be down somewhere in Chhamrachh village."

Replied Meena sir.

I did not take him seriously as I was too tired to use my mind after a long bus journey and was yet to reach the rooms of my colleagues. Sub Staff who was named Kashi Prasad Vishwakarma had affair with numerous ladies of Chhamrachh village and he was even considered to be secret father of several kids there. As soon as we reached their room, I was once again disappointed to see that there was no attached bathroom and there were not many options to live in this small village either. In order to use the bathroom, I had to carry my clothes and other belongings then walk over 100 meters and cross the farm of the landlord then use the washrooms. The only positive thing for me was not having to pay the rent as being an officer, bank pays your lease rent.

As we reached the room, both of them started preparing for dinner. I was extremely tired after a long day and as soon as I got fresh and found a bed to rest, I slept immediately.

I don't know for how long I was asleep, but it was Rai Ji who woke me up asking me to have dinner. I was hungry and sleepy as well. I joined the branch on 1st of May 2013 and Singrauli gets really hot in summers. There was only one fan and no cooler in the room or branch either, forget about airconditioner. I was cursing myself to have quit my job in SBB. I had everything there, it was close from my hometown, airconditioned bank premises, limited working hours, friends to go out and everything, but still I chose to leave it all for this. Suddenly I started hating everyone who encouraged me to go for this promotion including Rasika. Somehow, I slept that night and then joined the bank with two of my new colleagues about whom I did not know much about. I was missing Rasika and my mom badly, and I did not know when I will be able to see their faces again.

Dukh Dard Peeda and Some Lessons

Next day as I stood amidst the dusty streets of Nigri Niwas village, a sense of overwhelming sadness and nervousness washed over me. The village lacked even the most basic facilities, and the bank branch where I was assigned seemed like a world away from the bustling urban branches I had imagined. There were no guards to protect the bank, and the number of customers far outnumbered the available resources. It was a daunting sight, and tears welled up in my eyes as I realized the difficulty level of the challenges ahead.

With a heavy heart, I reached for my phone and dialed Rasika's number since I could not talk to her yesterday because of being so exhausted. As the phone rang, my heart pounded in my chest, and when she finally answered, her voice was a soothing balm to my troubled soul.

"Hey, Mayank. Is everything okay?"

Rasika's voice was filled with concern as she sensed the despair in my tone.

"Rasika, I… I don't know where to start,"

I began, my voice trembling with emotion.

"This village, it's nothing like I expected. There are no facilities, no guards at the bank, and the workload is overwhelming. I feel so lost and helpless."

Rasika listened attentively, her heart aching for me as she absorbed the gravity of the situation.

"Oh, Mayank, I had no idea it was this bad,"

She replied, her voice filled with shock and empathy.

"I can't imagine how difficult it must be for you."

Tears streamed down my cheeks as I poured out my frustrations and fears to her, finding solace in her unwavering support.

"I just don't know if I can handle this, Rasika. It's so different from what I'm used to, and I feel so out of place,"

I confessed; my voice choked with emotion.

Rasika's voice was a comforting presence on the other end of the line.

"Mayank, listen to me," she said, her tone gentle but firm.

"You're stronger than you think, and you have the resilience to overcome any obstacle that comes your way.

Remember why you chose this path in the first place and hold on to that."

Her words struck hard, igniting a flicker of determination amidst the despair.

"You're right, Rasika. I can't let this defeat me,"

I replied, feeling a renewed sense of resolve wash over me.

"Thank you for always being there for me, for believing in me even when I doubt myself."

Rasika's voice was filled with warmth and love as she reassured me, "I'll always be here for you, Mayank, no matter what. Together, we'll get through this."

And as we said our goodbyes, I felt a glimmer of hope flicker in my heart, knowing that with Rasika by my side, I could face whatever challenges lay ahead in Nigri Niwas village.

Time went by slowly in Singrauli and concurrently, I connected with Mr. Meena, discovering the unique insights he brought from the roots in Rajasthan. Conversations with him and Rai Sir, delved into the banking landscape specific to the village and the challenges faced by both customers and bank personnel. Through these exchanges, I gained an understanding of the cultural and economic factors influencing banking operations in this area.

Living and working in such a rural place is nothing like working in metros or urban areas. Here people you live or work with are also the people you spend most time with while in cities once you leave office there is hardly any connect.

As I settled into my new life in Singrauli, I found myself unexpectedly sharing a living space with two of my colleagues – Meena sir and Happy sir. Despite the initial awkwardness of living with near-strangers, I soon discovered that they were not just roommates, but also my mentors in bank as well as in the culinary arts. As we gradually settled into our shared living arrangement, discussions expanded beyond the professional life. In our daily interactions, we navigated the challenges of adapting to a new work environment while also accommodating diverse lifestyles. From meal preferences to daily routines, each aspect of our shared living space became an opportunity for understanding and respecting differences.

Initially unacquainted with cooking, I found myself in the capable hands of Meena sir and Happy sir, who generously shared their culinary expertise. The kitchen became a hub of cultural exchange, as Meena sir introduced recipes influenced by the vibrant flavors of Rajasthan, while Happy sir brought forth the culinary delights of Lucknow.

When I was living in hostel, the labour was divided and I was given this task of making Dal Fry and hence, it was the only dish which I could cook. Making Roti or Chapati was one of the tasks I found difficult and here Meena sir taught me how exactly to make round shape soft rotis.

One evening, as we gathered in the kitchen to prepare dinner, Meena sir and Happy sir exchanged mischievous glances, a twinkle of amusement in their eyes. I couldn't help but feel a sense of apprehension – what cooking adventure were they planning for me tonight?

"So, Mayank," Meena sir began,

"Today, we shall embark upon a culinary journey like no other – the art of making the perfect omelette!"

I blinked in surprise, unsure whether to be excited or terrified about it.

"Um, okay. I've never really cooked it before, but I'm willing to give it a try," I replied tentatively, eyeing the eggs and vegetables laid out on the counter.

Happy sir chuckled, his laughter filling the room. "Don't worry, Mayank. Cooking is like riding a bicycle – you might stumble a few times, but eventually, you'll get the hang of it."

And so, under the watchful guidance of my newfound mentors, I embarked upon my first attempt into the world of cooking an omlette. As Meena sir cracked eggs with practiced precision and Happy sir chopped vegetables with lightning speed, I fumbled awkwardly, sending bits of eggshell flying in all directions.

"Oops, looks like we have a rookie in the kitchen!" Meena sir teased.

I flushed with embarrassment, but laughter bubbled up inside me, dispelling the tension in the room.

"Sir, Rome wasn't built in a day!"

I replied, determined to prove that I was up to the challenge.

And so, with much laughter and good-natured banter, we embarked upon the task at hand. Meena sir demonstrated the delicate art of flipping an omelette with finesse, while Happy sir told us tales of his culinary misadventures – from burnt toast disasters to exploding pressure cookers.

As the aroma of sizzling eggs filled the air, I couldn't help but feel a sense of pride at the dish taking shape before me. Sure, it might not be the most perfect omelette in the world, but it was made with love and laughter – the secret ingredients that truly make a meal special.

And as we sat down to enjoy our meal, I couldn't help but feel grateful for the unexpected friendships and cooking lessons that life had brought my way. Who knew that a simple omelette could hold so much laughter, joy, and camaraderie? As I took a bite, savoring the delicious flavors, I knew that this was just the beginning of many more culinary adventures to come.

While we were having taste of the omlette, our conversation turned to a hot topic that had captured the nation's attention in April 2013 – the Indian Premier League (IPL) spot-fixing scandal.

"Did you hear about the latest developments in the IPL scandal?"

Meena sir asked, his eyebrows rose in concern.

Happy sir nodded affirmatively, his expression mirroring the gravity of the situation. "Yes, it's quite shocking to see such corruption in our beloved cricket league," he replied, carefully stirring the curry on the stove.

"It's disheartening to think that players and officials would stoop to such levels for personal gain," I remarked, flipping the next omelette.

And so, as we cooked and talked, our conversation served as a reminder of the importance of honesty, integrity, and fair play – not just in sports, but in all aspects of life. And as we sat down to enjoy our meal, I couldn't help but feel grateful for the opportunity to share such meaningful discussions with my newfound friends.

Even though we enjoyed cooking together, but there were days when the prospect of cooking after a long day at work seemed daunting.

The absence of external dining options in Nagri Niwas also meant that willingly or unwillingly we must cook every day for ourselves. In a village where restaurants were scarce, we confronted the reality that our kitchen was not merely a place of choice but a necessity. The limitations of dining out created a sense of shared responsibility, fostering a mutual understanding that cooking together was not just a preference but a practical and essential part of our daily routine.

Through perseverance, humor, and a collective acknowledgment of the practicalities of our situation, I, Meena sir, and Happy sir created bonds that crossed the boundaries of our roles, creating a home away from home within the walls of Nagri Niwas.

As I settled into my role, I began to see beyond the initial discomforts. The absence of air conditioning transformed into an appreciation for the simplicity of the village life. The ambient noise, rather than being a distraction, became the soundtrack of community engagement. The lack of ventilation was overshadowed by the genuine warmth of the villagers who had embraced me as one of their own.

My journey into Nagri Niwas was not just a professional assignment; it was a transformative experience that challenged my preconceptions and expanded the understanding of banking beyond transactional processes. The absence of modern conveniences, far from being a hindrance, became a testament to the resilience of the villagers and the richness of rural life.

In navigating the crowded, noisy, and fragrant rural branch, I found not only the challenges of remote banking but also the opportunities to make a meaningful impact in the lives of the villagers.

Navigating the challenges of remote banking in Nagri Niwas also meant grappling with limited technological infrastructure, irregular power supply, and the nuances of a community deeply rooted in its traditions.

My daily routine involved not just managing financial transactions but also engaging in conversations with the villagers, understanding their needs, and tailoring banking solutions that resonated with the local context.

Journey to Nagri Niwas, though marked by uncertainties, became a testament to the resilience and adaptability required in the world of remote banking. The rustic landscapes and the simplicity of rural life offered not just challenges but a unique canvas for me to redefine the role of a banker in the context of a remote Indian village. As I continued to navigate the winding roads and build connections in Nagri Niwas, I found that the true essence of my journey extended beyond banking transactions – it was a transformative experience that blurred the lines between professionalism and community, urbanity and remoteness.

Legend of Kashi and Budhsen

My first encounter with the legendry sub staffs of the Nagri Niwas branch painted a picture of stark contrasts. I still remember when I first saw Kashi Prasad Vishwakarma who was the famous peon of this branch as he was renowned in whole Rewa Region. The air around Kashi Prasad reeked of the intense odor of alcohol, and his appearance spoke volumes about his lifestyle. He had a big mustache which local ladies were fond of and in local bagheli language they used to call him "Mechha" because of his mustache. He always wore white pant and white shirt so whenever travelling in train, half of the railway staff thought of him as staff of railways and others believed him to be in army because of the mustache. Because of this benefit of doubt, he never purchased ticket while travelling in train.

"Good morning, sir. You must be the new officer. I'm Kashi Prasad, the peon around here. Need anything, just let me know," Kashi Prasad introduced himself with alcohol trailed his every word.

Though taken aback by the unprofessionalism, I nodded politely, "Thank you, Kashi Prasad. I'm here to work together and serve the community. Let's make sure we provide the best service to the villagers."

"Do not worry much as you will not be able to change much."

"Sahab bank me do hi aadmi hote hain ek sabse bada (branch manager) aur ek sabse chhota (Peon) beech wale sab pelar hote hain."

Kashi Prasad, seemingly unfazed by my words, merely replied and stumbled away, leaving me to ponder the complexities of working with such a character.

As I delved further into the branch, my attention turned to Budhsen, the record keeper. Budhsen, known for his crazy behavior, sat hunched over a pile of papers, his eyes vacant and distant. I approached him cautiously, aware of the unique challenges presented by this half-mad record keeper.

"Good morning, Budhsen. I'm Mayank Sharma, the new officer. How are you doing?" I inquired, trying to establish a connection.

Budhsen, his gaze unfocused, mumbled before breaking into a fit of laughter. This was so unusual, and I felt strange and little afraid too. I did not know how to deal with him and Kashi as well. Sub staffs are extremely important in a branch because we can only run the counter while all other supporting tasks are performed by the peon and record keeper. Here in this branch both of them were out of our control. Uncertain about how to navigate this situation, I decided to approach it with patience and empathy.

Over the next few days, I observed the dynamics within the branch. Kashi Prasad's erratic behavior continued, with instances of verbal abuse directed at customers becoming an unfortunate norm. I realized that addressing this issue required a delicate balance – since I was new to this branch and even the existing staff working from years in the branch usually avoided getting in arguments with him.

Budhsen was mentally not well and was definitely not fit for this job as record keeping was in extremely poor condition. His son Kamlesh used to come and help him in keeping daily vouchers since he along with his stepmother and stepsister were all still connected with Budhsen because he was earning. Such is life; money was the base of their relationship. They all hated Budhsen and maybe Budhsen also knew this, but this is how they were living. Budhsen was a heavy drinker as his style of drinking was very unusual and unique for me. There was this local alcoholic drink which they used to call Lal Wali. Budhsen will go with a Lota in his hand and get it filled from the local vendor, offering him a cheque from his salary account and then drink the whole Lota full of Lal wali in one go. And within minutes, he will fall flat on ground. Such was the effect of this local drink.

One day, as I approached Kashi Prasad and chose a more direct approach, "Kashi Prasad, the behavior towards customers needs to change. We are here to serve them, not make their experience unpleasant."

Kashi Prasad, seemingly unapologetic, replied in a dismissive tone, "They don't know anything. I've been running this place just fine. Why fix something that isn't broken?"

"I have been providing several services to them, which you may never imagine. Let me make a call and you will see."

He took out his phone and dialled some number. It was a lady from chhamrachh village.

"Hello, you wanted the passbook, right?" he spoke in local Bagheli language.

"Yes, shall I come to the bank?"

The lady replied.

"Yes, you take your passbook, and I will take what is mine".

He boldly asked for an act which was very shameful for the bank. But to my surprise, the lady smiled and agreed to his demand. I just could not understand what was happening in this village which I felt was 20 years behind the world.

I tried to explain the importance of professional conduct and customer satisfaction. While Kashi Prasad remained resistant, I knew that cultivating a positive work culture would require persistent efforts.

Simultaneously, I sought to understand Budhsen's situation better. I learned that Budhsen, once a competent record keeper, because of the pressures of rural life had turned to alcohol as a coping mechanism after his first wife who was the mother of Kamlesh died.

"Budhsen, I see that you're facing challenges. Is there anything I can do to help or support you?" I asked, choosing a compassionate approach.

Budhsen, in a moment of clarity, shared fragments of his struggles and the loneliness he felt.

Over time, my efforts bore fruit. Kashi Prasad, influenced by the positive changes around him, started mending his ways solwly. The atmosphere within the branch began to shift, and even Budhsen showed signs of improvement as external support systems were put in place.

Typical Day in Kala Pani Branch

In the heart of Singrauli, I found myself navigating the challenges of a branch overwhelmed by the aspirations and demands of over 200 villagers. Nagri Niwas branch was also called as Kala Pani Branch by the authorities sitting at Zonal Office Bhopal and I came to know this fact when I went for my induction training later. This place was a hell for bankers working here and it was a punishment posting where officer having done misconduct were placed and new recruits like me were posted for training.

Working in Nagri Niwas was extremely tough not just because this was remotely located but also because 90% of the customers were illiterate. Understanding their problems in their typical Bagheli language and then explaining them the solution with bank's method and practices in a language which they understood was a humongous task. They hardly understood what I said to them and often I had to take help of Kamlesh or Kashi to make them understand. Whole day I had to shout out loud to keep things under control.

Every day I began my day with a sense of purpose, ready to serve the community. However, as the doors swung open, a wave of villagers entered the branch. The hustle and bustle became more than a routine; it transformed into a symphony of voices, each carrying the weight of financial problems and expectations.

Our branch was the only bank available in 48 villages and was also the leading bank of the district. It also meant that customer base was huge but having such large numbers of illiterate customers literally sucked all our energy.

The counters, manned by me and my colleagues, remained the epicenter of financial transactions right from the morning. Villagers, diverse in age and background, queue up with variety of tasks – from simple deposits to complex loan applications. The sense of urgency was palpable, and I felt the pressure building as I strived to address the needs of each customer.

The sheer volume of footfall transformed the once-spacious branch into a crowded arena. The air became charged with impatience and caught in the whirlwind of demands; I grappled with the challenge of prioritizing tasks. Each villager believed their transaction was of utmost importance, creating a dynamic where time became a precious commodity.

Seated behind the counter, I juggled between customer queries which had huge variety.

At any given time, there were more than 50 customers who just wanted to know the balance in their account. Government of India and state government provide numerous financial benefits to the society and living in cities, we hardly come to know about those schemes. In a village like Niwas, most people are illiterate and below poverty line having no source of income and therefore these schemes are the support system for the most basic human needs. Half the task was done once the balance enquiry information was given to them. Kashi had this duty to maintain the line and discipline in the branch, but he was mostly not available. I had to shout and arrange the line and then collect passbooks of everyone who wanted to know their bank balance. I used to collect more than 50 passbooks at once and instruct them to maintain silence and listen to their names when I call. There was no guard in the branch and more often than not the peon and Daftari were absent. From cleaning our own desks to maintaining lines and discipline and dealing with more than 500 customers every day in a premises where there was no air conditioning, washroom or water supply, we were asked to work in such pathetic conditions and yes, I did it for the three and a half years of my life.

The frustration generally mounted not only within me but among the villagers as well. The limited resources and infrastructure of the branch amplified the challenges. The absence of adequate seating arrangements, coupled with the continuous influx of people, created an environment which was both physically and mentally testing. Striving to maintain professionalism, I battled the suffocating atmosphere while attempting to provide efficient service.

The branch building had no ventilation, so in a small hall having no air-conditioning with more than 200 people inside at once and more customers standing outside, our branch was so suffocating that incident of fainting of lady or older customers was not uncommon. We could not do anything about it and yes there was no washroom in the branch. Whenever I felt like it, I was forced to go outside find a place where there will not be anyone. Our clothes were wet with sweat throughout the day because of the extreme heat and when I say clothes, I also mean the undergarments. Sitting in such state and performing our duties with precision was no less than any Tapasya.

Some seek clarification on banking products, others needed assistance with digital services, and a significant number were there for routine transactions. The frustration in my eyes mirrored the impatience in the eyes of those waiting, creating a cycle of tension within the branch.

The frustration was not born out of a lack of willingness to serve but rather from the overwhelming demand that stretched the resources thin. Lunch breaks were a brief respite, allowing a moment of reprieve before plunging back into the sea of expectations.

Afternoons in the Singrauli branch often witnessed a surge in customers. The closing hours loom, and villagers, aware of the impending deadline, clamoured for attention. The pressure to meet the needs of the community clashed with the constraints of time and resources.

The frustration within the branch extended beyond the physical space. Staff of our branch faced the challenge of balancing professionalism with the emotional toll that comes with being at the forefront of financial interactions. The constant barrage of demands can lead to burnout, affecting not only the well-being of the employees but also the quality of service they provide.

Despite the frustrations, there was a sense of responsibility that grounded me. I understood the significance of the public sector bank in the lives of the villagers. The branch was not just a financial institution; it was a lifeline for the community, offering access to essential services that can transform lives. This realization became a source of motivation amid the challenges.

Every day at 4 PM when we closed the gate; more than a hundred of people were already inside the premises and almost same number of customers were waiting outside. It was extremely difficult for us to manage such large number of customers. Opening and closing of gates for regular exit of customers in the evening always led to fights. There was no guard for our protection or for the safety of bank. Peon was always missing either making illegal money through bribe or going after lady customers.

And yes, after such hectic days which was routine, we had to go back and cook for ourselves. Those were some really tough days in my banking career.

Chapter VII

Echoes of Empathy

As I delved deeper into my role at the Nagri Niwas branch, I began to uncover the harsh reality of the villagers' lives. The customers who walked through the branch's doors were individuals grappling with the challenges of extreme poverty.

The stark contrast between the urban branch I had previously worked or seen in Barhi and the rural reality of Nagri Niwas was profound. The customers here were not seeking complex financial solutions or investment advice; rather, their transactions were lifelines – small sums of money to sustain daily existence, to weather the uncertainties of agricultural cycles, or to address urgent healthcare needs.

Walking through the narrow lanes of Nagri Niwas, I witnessed the huts made of mud and thatch, the barefoot children playing in the dust, and the elderly faces etched with the lines of resilience. Each interaction with a customer became a reminder of the immense challenges they faced.

The financial transactions, often minuscule in monetary terms, carried immense weight in the lives of the customers. A modest loan for a farmer meant the possibility of sowing seeds for the next crop; a small withdrawal for a mother might translate into a day's meal for her children. Viewing these transactions through the lens of social impact, I felt a profound sense of responsibility to facilitate these small yet significant changes.

The joy I derived from serving the people of Nagri Niwas went beyond the conventional measures of success. It wasn't about meeting sales targets or achieving high transaction volumes; it was about the palpable impact on individual lives. The smiles of gratitude from a farmer who could now afford seeds, the relief in the eyes of a mother who could provide a warm meal to her children – these were the moments that fueled my sense of purpose.

The villagers, initially skeptical of a newcomer, began to see me not just as a banker but as a partner in their journey towards economic stability. The transformation within the community mirrored the transformation within me – from banking professional to a compassionate advocate for social change.

It was 5:50 PM and gate of the branch was closed as today being a local festival, there were less number of customers yet it was another hectic day and we hardly got a second to rest. After finishing the cash transactions and accepting all the account opening forms, Kashi got all the customers out of the premises and closed the door. I was having a bad headache and just wanted some fresh air, so I went out. I was standing outside and saw an old lady sitting outside the branch. It was the month of November and even though we did not feel the cold inside the branch premises, I felt the dropping temperature as I went out. The old lady was alone, so I was curious to know why she was still sitting there when branch business operations were closed.

"Amma why are you sitting here? Branch is closed now."

I asked her.

"Babuji my village is 29 KM from here and I came here in the morning walking along with my fellow villagers; they all got their money and went back. I could not reach to the cash counter and never realized that bank will be closed after 4 PM. I don't know how I will go back now."

She replied almost crying.

I took her passbook and asked,

"How much money did you want to withdraw?"

"Sahab government gives monthly pension of Rs 300. I came here to withdraw that amount only." She replied innocently.

I was stunned to know that she walked all the way 29 KM just to withdraw Rs 300 from her account. I went inside and checked her account balance and was shocked and heartbroken at the same time to know that her pension was not credited yet. I did not have courage to tell this to her, so I just pretended to take her thumb impression on a withdrawal form and gave her Rs 300.

She was so happy to finally receive the money and gave me blessings. I still remember her face and the smile she had. This was one of the happiest moments of my stay in Nagri Niwas. Another example of how making others happy is the ultimate secret to real happiness.

In the quiet moments after the branch closed its doors for the day, as I reflected on the impact of my work, I realized that the pleasure derived from serving the people of Nagri Niwas wasn't just professional satisfaction; it was a profound sense of fulfillment that transcended the boundaries of a banking career. The role that began as a social experiment evolved into a testament to the power of empathy, resilience, and the transformative potential of humble acts of service in the face of poverty. Through commitment to social work disguised as banking, I found a purpose that resonated with the beating heart of rural India.

Gone Case of Helmet Chase

Recently another branch in Tikri village which was only 8 kilometeres away from Niwas was opened. A new staff Anil had joined as a clerk in Tikri branch and shared the same building with us. Now, let me tell you about Anil. He was a nice guy, always cheerful, but he had one little quirk - he had a huge crush on a beautiful staff nurse who recently joined the government hospital in our village.

Every day, like clockwork, Anil would spot the nurse and his heart will start beating faster. He would try to gather all his courage to talk to her, but alas, his tongue always seemed to tie itself into knots whenever she was around. Poor Anil!

Now, here's where things got a bit funny. One day, Anil came up with what he thought was a brilliant plan to get the nurse's attention. He decided to wear a helmet to hide his face and then chase after her as she walked around the village. Yes, you heard me right - a helmet!

So, picture this: there's Anil, wearing a helmet that's way too big for his head, running after the nurse like a clumsy puppy, sometimes he even chased her in a bicycle, wearing that big helmet. You can imagine the sight! People passing by would stop and stare, wondering what on earth was going on. Some even thought it was some sort of new village entertainment!

But did the nurse notice Anil's efforts? Well, let's just say she definitely noticed, but perhaps not in the way Anil had hoped. Instead of being impressed from his romantic gesture, she simply ignored him, or worse, she laughed! Poor Anil's heart sank every time.

Despite the embarrassment, Anil was undeterred. He was determined to win the nurse's heart, even if it meant making a fool of himself in the process. And so, day after day, he would wear his helmet and continue his pursuit, much to the amusement of everyone around him.

But you know what they say - love makes you do crazy things. And for Anil, wearing a helmet and chasing after the nurse was just his way of showing how much he cared. Who knows, maybe one day his persistence would pay off, and he'd finally get the girl of his dreams.

As the days went by, Anil's helmet adventures became the talk of the village. People would gather on the streets, eagerly waiting for the daily spectacle to unfold. Some even started placing bets on whether Anil would finally catch the nurse's attention or if he would trip over his own feet first!

But despite the laughs and the teasing, Anil remained undeterred. He was a man on a mission, determined to win over the nurse's heart no matter what it took. And so, he continued his daily routine of wearing the helmet and chasing after her, his determination matched only by his clumsiness.

One day, as Anil was in hot pursuit of the nurse, disaster struck. His shoelaces came undone, causing him to trip and fall flat on his face, helmet rolling off in the process. The whole village erupted into laughter, including the nurse, who couldn't help but giggle at the sight.

Embarrassed and red-faced, Anil picked himself up and dusted himself off, determined not to let this setback weaken his spirits. With his amazing determination, he put the helmet back on and continued his pursuit, much to the amusement of the onlookers.

As the weeks passed, Anil's antics became a part of village lore. But amidst all the laughter and the jokes, there was a glimmer of hope in Anil's eyes. Despite the countless rejections and the countless falls, he refused to give up on his dream of winning the nurse's heart. And who knows, maybe one day his perseverance would pay off, and he'd finally get his happily ever after.

Until then, Anil would continue to wear his helmet and chase after the nurse, his determination as unwavering as ever. And as for the rest of villagers, they'd continue to cheer him on from the sidelines, eager to see what hilarious antics he'd come up with next. After all, life in Niwas village was never dull, especially with characters like Anil around!

The Lost Chequebook

Our branch operations were paused, and trust was shattered one day when a customer reported the theft of his cheque book and the subsequent unauthorized withdrawals from his account. Shockwaves went through all the staff as the severity of the situation unfolded. We immediately initiated a thorough inquiry to unearth the truth behind this unfortunate incident. Such an incident was new to us as it had never happened in past.

The customer expressed not only financial loss but also a breach of trust that extended beyond mere transactions. He also threatened to file a police complaint, casting a shadow over the reputation of the branch and its commitment to safeguarding customers' interests.

The very foundation of the branch's integrity was at stake and resolving the matter swiftly and transparently became utmost important.

The initial stages of the investigation led to a startling revelation – Kamlesh, the son of Budhsen, the record keeper, was involved in the theft and fraudulent transactions. The realization sent shockwaves through the branch, as Kamlesh was not only an insider but also part of the close-knit community.

"Oh no, this is a big problem. Budhsen's negligence has put us all in a tight spot." I was discussing it with Happy sir.

Happy sir: I can't believe this happened. Budhsen was always drunk and never realized when in the pretext of helping, Kamlesh did this. But his mistake has caused a lot of trouble.

"We need to figure out how to fix this mess. The customer's money has been stolen, and it's our responsibility to make it right sir." I was concerned

Happy: But what about Budhsen? He may lose his job over this, and he didn't mean for any of this to happen.

"I know sir, but we have to prioritize the customer's safety and trust in the bank. We'll support Budhsen through this, but we also need to make sure something like this never happens again." I was also concerned about Budhsen's job.

Happy: You're right, Mayank. We'll have to tighten our security measures and make sure every employee understands the importance of keeping sensitive information safe. Security items including all cheque books are under Meena sir's custody.

"Absolutely sir. Let's focus on resolving this issue first and then work on preventing it from happening in the future. Budhsen may have made a mistake, but we're a team, and we'll get through this together." I replied.

Grappling with a complex mix of emotions, we knew that addressing the situation required both sensitivity and firm action. The customer's trust had been violated, and the reputation of the branch hung in the balance.

It was such a coincidence that our branch was not having any branch manager since no one joined after the previous branch head was transferred after it came to the knowledge of regional office that he used to consume alcohol during working hours and our accountant Mr. Meena was also on leave to visit his home that day. Cheque books were under the custody of Meena sir and therefore he was directly responsible for this loss. Approaching the customer, I offered a sincere apology for the unfortunate incident and assured him that every effort would be made to rectify the situation. He was a government schoolteacher and used to withdraw his monthly salary through chequebook. There was no ATM in our branch and in fact there was no ATM anywhere around 40 KM range. I explained the steps being taken to investigate the matter and committed to providing him with a detailed account of the findings.

Simultaneously, I had a candid conversation with Budhsen about his son's involvement in the fraudulent activities. The revelation left Budhsen visibly distraught, torn between familial loyalty and the professional integrity that defined the ethos of the branch.

"Ji saab Ji Ji Ji Ji Ji Ji Ji."

He literally said this to me; actually, it was his way of communicating. This series of 'Ji' was typical Budhsen giving affirmation about anything and everything.

Recognizing the delicate nature of the situation, I assured Budhsen that the matter would be handled impartially, with the focus on justice and accountability. The branch's commitment to transparency and ethical conduct had to prevail over personal relationships.

As the investigation progressed, evidence against Kamlesh mounted. The extent of the fraudulent activities, the withdrawal of significant sums from multiple branches, painted a disheartening picture. Poor Budhsen who was not aware of his son's greedy intentions, understood the severity of the situation and rallied behind our efforts to address it promptly.

Our team somehow confronted Kamlesh with the evidence. The admission of guilt was accompanied by a mix of remorse and justifications that revealed the complex web of personal issues that had led to such a betrayal of trust. Kamlesh was unemployed and was working in our branch to support his father. He also loved a girl whom he wished to marry but everything requires money. His father Budhsen earned well since he was very senior, and his salary was good enough to provide a family. But, his second wife, who was not Kamlesh's mother, kept the chequebook of salary account of Budhsen and used to withdraw all the money as soon as the salary was credited every month. Ultimately Kamlesh did not get any pocket money, so he planned this along with some of his notorious friends.

Facing the victimized customer, we ensured a fair and transparent resolution. The branch, acknowledging its responsibility in the security lapse, committed to compensating the customer for the financial losses incurred and implementing enhanced security measures to prevent such incidents in the future. Even though I was not in the picture but all of us decided to equally bear the loss and collected the money and reimbursed the customer.

As the branch worked to restore the customer's trust, our team faced the challenge of dealing with Kamlesh's actions within the confines of the law. The customer, though initially adamant about involving the police, was ultimately convinced by the branch's sincerity in addressing the matter.

In a final conversation with the customer, we expressed genuine regret for the inconvenience he had endured. He reiterated the branch's commitment to learning from the incident and enhancing security protocols to prevent a recurrence.

The resolution of the incident became a turning point for the Nagri Niwas branch. The incident had tested the team's resilience and commitment to ethical conduct, but it also reinforced the importance of transparency, accountability, and customer-centricity.

A Nurse's Proposal

It was February 2014, and I was about to complete one year in Nagri Niwas branch. One fine day in the midst of the daily banking routine at branch, my world took an unexpected turn when I found myself at the center of an unconventional proposal. A nurse, presumably a customer of the bank, handed me a letter along with a beautiful rose expressing her feelings. As I unfold the letter, mix emotion of amusement and anger flooded inside me.

I was sitting at the account opening counter and she used to visit branch frequently for opening of accounts of members of Self-Help Group. The letter written in Bagheli language read,

"Dear Sirji. Ever since you have joined this bank, I have always adored you. I really like you and love you so much. Please accept my proposal and if you feel the same just keep this rose."

The nurse's feelings, expressed in a neatly folded letter, added a surreal layer to my routine. The bank premises, usually busy with financial transactions and customer interactions, became the backdrop for an unexpected romantic twist. As I read the heartfelt words penned by the nurse, my initial reaction was a burst of laughter as the situation striked me very comical.

Amusement, however, quickly gave way to anger as I realised that this may lead to trouble and is also hindering my personal space. The branch, a space dedicated to financial transactions and community service, now became an unexpected arena for matters of the heart.

Her name was Shalini Sahu and her letter filled with expressions of admiration and affection, became a paradoxical document in my hands. The emotions play out in a complex dance within my mind as I was trying to find the appropriate course of action.

She sat there the whole day even though her account opening form was submitted already. She was watching me the whole time and when someone is doing so, you eventually come to notice it. As I interacted with customers and addressed their financial needs, I couldn't shake the feeling of being watched or the knowledge that my every move was now viewed through a different lens.

As the day progressed, I contemplated how to address the situation. The anger that initially rose began to transform into a more measured response – a realization that open communication may be the key to resolving this unforeseen complication.

The nurse, perhaps unaware of the impact her gesture has had on me, continued with her efforts. In a moment of introspection, I decided to approach the matter with a candid conversation. During lunch break, I called Shalini to a quiet corner of the branch, away from the prying eyes and curious gazes.

"Why have you given this letter to me?"

I asked politely.

"Is there any misunderstanding?"

I continued.

She just looked at me and smiled. Realizing that my direct approach was being misunderstood by her, I took a little rude approach.

"I am not the kind of guy who accepts such random proposals."

"I respect your feelings Shalini ji, but I do not feel the same for you. I cannot accept this rose please keep it with you."

I cleared my intentions to her.

The conversation that ensued was awkward yet necessary. I expressed my gratitude for her feelings and acknowledged the sincerity behind the letter. However, I candidly communicated the discomfort which I felt and returned her rose. The nurse, taken aback by the directness of the conversation, listened to me with a mix of embarrassment and understanding.

"Sorry sirji."

That was all she said to me and left.

In the aftermath of this exchange, a sense of relief washed over me. The nurse, though initially disheartened, appreciated the honesty and respected my need for professional boundaries. My interactions with customers resumed their usual focus on financial matters, and the nurse, though still a customer became a part of the daily ebb and flow.

The experience left me with a newfound awareness of the delicate balance between professional and personal spheres. The laughter that initially erupted from the unconventional proposal now turned into a reflective smile – a recognition of the unpredictability that life can bring, even within the small premises of a public sector bank in Singrauli.

Heartfelt Reunion

It's been more than a month since I last met Rasika and I had started missing her badly. This was the first time in our relationship that we had not seen each other for this long. I informed Rasika about coming to Jabalpur and she eagerly awaited my arrival at the station. The moment I steped off the train, our eyes met, and smiles exchanged the unspoken joy of being together again. She was waiting outside Jabalpur railway station for me in her scooty. As soon as I saw her, I waved my hands in the air.

"Hi babe."

She said while hugging me.

"Hello Jaan. I missed you badly."

I replied tightening the hug.

"Missed you too."

She expressed her feeling as well.

This was our routine, whenever I came to Jabalpur, she will come and pick me up from the railway station and then we will roam around together. The day unfolded with a plan to watch the movie "X-Men," yet little did we know that the real story will unfold in the corners of the cinema, where love takes center stage.

As we left the station, the energy between us was palpable. She was driving her scooty and I was sitting very close behind her. Rasika, with an endearing smile, suggested watching "X-Men" as a way to spend quality time together. We booked ticket in South Avenue Mall which was then the biggest mall of the city and the best place to watch a movie.

The cinema, with its dimly lit hall and the scent of buttered popcorn in the air, became the sanctuary where I and Rasika decide to immerse ourselves in the magic of storytelling.

As we entered the cinema, the anticipation of the movie's storyline was overshadowed by the anticipation of being close to each other. With the ticket in hand, we found our way to a corner seat. We always booked corner seats since it was the safest and the best place to spend some quality time together.

As the opening scenes of "X-Men" unfolded, we found ourselves entranced not by the tale of superheroes but by the chemistry that simmered between us.

In the darkness of the cinema hall, our hands found each other, fingers intertwining in a dance of familiarity and affection. The darkness became a canvas for stolen kisses and whispered words. The corner seat, initially chosen for its seclusion, transformed into a private place of shared intimacy.

She was wearing a one piece and was looking so pretty. Dark corner of the theater and her closeness with that seductive perfume was making me go crazy. I could not help but put my hands on her thighs and gradually pulled the dress up. She was nervous but was feeling the heat as we continued with the kissing.

"I love you Rasika."

I said while still feeling the warmth of her body. Romancing in public places gave both of us a little more excitement and we enjoyed it a lot. The corner seat shielded us from the outside world, allowing time to stand still in the midst of unfolding frames.

Those romantic moments did not diminish the magic of "X-Men"; rather, they enhanced it. In the midst of stolen kisses and shared whispers, we lost track of the movie's narrative. The popcorn, untouched, served as a testament to our focus on each other rather than the cinematic plot unfolding before us. The cinema hall, filled with the echoes of the film's soundtrack, became a haven for unspoken affections.

"I love you Rasika. I really do."

I expressed my love looking deeply in her eyes.

"I love you too Mayank."

She replied and I did not miss the moment and kissed her lips again.

The corner seat, initially chosen for its discreetness, became a stage for a dance of emotions.

As the movie neared its conclusion, I and Rasika, still entwined in each other's arms, realized that our day in

Jabalpur has been more about the life we shared than the fictional X-Men. The closing scenes of the film served as a backdrop to our own reflections on love, companionship, and the beauty of finding solace in each other's presence.

Exiting the cinema, hand in hand, we carried with ourselves the echoes of shared moments. After the movie, we went to 70 MM which was one of our favourite restaurants to have lunch. Then we strolled through the city, sharing anecdotes and laughter.

The streets of Jabalpur, now bathed in the glow of streetlights, witnessed the continuation of our love story. The day that began with a reunion at the station and a plan to watch "X-Men" culminated in a realization – that the magic of our connection transcends the confined of any cinematic narrative.

As the night deepened, we found ourselves at a charming café, where we extended our day with conversations that bridged the gap between the cinematic and the real.

Finally, it was getting late and my train, Shaktipunj Express, to Singrauli was scheduled at 11:50 from Jabalpur Railways station. Since Rasika could not stay out till those late hours, I asked her to drop me at the railway station by 9 PM. It was time for me to go back and it was always painful to say goodbye to her. Both of us wanted this day to last longer as this was one of the few days in a month when we actually find time to see and meet each other. I hugged her and asked her to leave as she was about to cry, and I could not see that. As soon as she left, I plugged in my headphone, and can you guess the song I played on my phone? Yes, it was Aadat.

Caught in the Act

Living in Niwas village as a bank officer was usually peaceful, but one Sunday, everything changed. My colleagues decided to have a party in our building. My room was in the same building, and my mother was visiting and staying with me those days. Little did I know, this day would become one of the most embarrassing moments of my life.

It all started innocently enough. My colleagues including Rai sir, Branch manager sir and few others had gathered, and someone cracked open a beer. It was the month of May and heat was at its peak. Soon, more drinks followed—vodka, whiskey, and all sorts of liquor. As the hours passed, the atmosphere grew rowdier, and the drinks kept flowing. I joined in, thinking it would be fun. I used to consume alcoholic drinks back then but was avoiding it ever since my mother had come to live with me.

As the party kicked off in, the air was filled with laughter and the clinking of glasses. We gathered around a makeshift table, where bottles of beer and spirits were lined up like soldiers ready for battle.

"Cheers to a day off!" Happy sir exclaimed, raising his glass in a toast. We all cheered and took a sip, the cold liquid soothing against the warmth of the afternoon sun.

The conversation flowed freely, punctuated by bursts of laughter and occasional shouts of excitement. We shared stories from work, traded jokes, and debated the latest news and gossip.

"Can you believe what happened at the branch last week?" one of my colleagues exclaimed, leaning in closer to the group. "I heard it was chaos!"

We all leaned in, eager to hear the juicy details. The conversation quickly turned animated as we discussed the events of the past week, each of us offering our own opinions and theories.

As the hours passed and the drinks kept flowing, the mood began to shift. The jokes became louder, the laughter got louder. Someone put on music, and soon we were dancing and singing along, our inhibitions fading with each passing moment.

I joined in the dance floor, feeling a sense of camaraderie with my colleagues. For a brief moment, I forgot about my responsibilities and the world outside. All that mattered was the here and now, the feeling of freedom and abandon.

But as the afternoon turned into evening, the effects of the alcohol began to take their toll. I felt a bit lightheaded, my movements a little unsteady. The room started to spin, and I struggled to focus on the conversations around me.

"Hey, are you okay?" one of my colleagues asked, noticing my dazed expression. I nodded, trying to brush off their concern. But deep down, I knew I had gone too far.

As the party continued to escalate, I found myself caught up in the chaos. I laughed too loudly, spoke too recklessly, and drank too much. And then, in a moment of madness, I broke a beer bottle in my hand.

The room fell silent as everyone turned to stare at me in shock. I felt a surge of panic and embarrassment, my cheeks burning with shame. I didn't know what to say or do—I just wanted to disappear.

"Hey, calm down, Mayank," one of my colleagues said, trying to diffuse the tension. But it was too late. The damage had been done, and I knew I had crossed a line.

I drank more than I should have, and before I knew it, I was acting strangely. My colleagues were startled and afraid. I didn't even recognize myself in that moment. Blood was everywhere and one of the colleagues tied a cotton bandage around the wound. I was not feeling the pain such is the effect of alcohol if consumed in that much quantity.

Suddenly, amidst the chaos, my mother appeared. She had somehow found out about the party as I was missing since Morning. Her face was filled with shock and anger. "What on earth do you think you're doing?" she exclaimed. However drunk you are my friend but when your mother is standing in front of you in such a situation, "Poori utar jati hai."

I was speechless, overwhelmed with shame. I had never wanted my mother to see me like this—out of control, drunk, and making a fool of myself. "I-I'm sorry, Mom," I stammered, unable to meet her gaze.

Her anger turned to disappointment. "I didn't raise you to behave like this," she said, her voice trembling with emotion. "I would rather see you dead than see you like this."

Those words hit me like a punch to the gut. I felt a wave of guilt wash over me. How had I let things get out of control like this? How had I disappointed the one person who had always believed in me?

My mother's words echoed in my mind as I retreated to my room, consumed by shame and regret. I knew I had let her down, and I knew I had let myself down. I couldn't bear to face anyone, not even myself.

The next day, I called in sick to work. I needed time to process what had happened, to come to terms with my actions. I spent the next two weeks holed up in my room, avoiding contact with the outside world.

During that time, I reflected on my behavior and the consequences of my actions. I realized that drinking had clouded my judgment and led me down a dangerous path. I knew I needed to make changes, not just for myself, but for the sake of my loved ones.

When I finally emerged from my self-imposed exile, I made a vow to myself. I would never let alcohol control me again. I would be more mindful of my actions and the impact they had on those around me.

It wasn't easy, but with time and determination, I was able to move past that dark moment in my life. I made amends with my mother, apologizing for my behavior and assuring her that I was committed to making positive changes.

Looking back on that day, I realize it was a wake-up call—a harsh reminder of the dangers of excess and the importance of self-control. It taught me a valuable lesson about responsibility and the power of choice.

I may have stumbled along the way, but I emerged stronger and wiser because of it. And for that, I am grateful.

Navigating Differences

After my return from Jabalpur from the last meeting when we watched X-men, I thought about the good time we had together. Even though everything seemed fine between us but there was something which bothered me. One fine day I was on a call with Rasika and we were discussing about future life and the prospect of marriage and the knowledge that our families may not readily embrace the union.

As we embarked on the journey of discussing our future, the difference in our cultural backgrounds became apparent. While I was from a Brahmin family, she belonged to the OBC community. The rich tapestry of Indian society, woven with diverse traditions and caste dynamics, added layers of complexity to our relationship. While love knows no boundaries, societal structures often impose constraints that demand negotiation and understanding.

Realizing the growing tension between us and the fear of losing her, I once again went to Jabalpur and met her in Indian Coffee House Sadar.

The Cafe provided a somber backdrop as we sat, tension hanging in the air like an unspoken truth. The weight of our conversation bore down on us, each word uttered carrying the gravity of uncertainty.

Mayank: (hesitant) We need to talk about our future, about us.

Rasika: (sighs) I know, Mayank. It's been on my mind too.

Mayank: (softly) My family, they're deeply rooted in traditions, you know that. The Brahmin identity means a lot to them.

Rasika: (nodding sadly) And mine… they have their own set of expectations. They might not understand our connection.

A heavy silence settled in, an unspoken acknowledgment of the obstacles we faced in bridging the cultural gap that stretched between us.

Mayank: (pauses) I love you, but the reality is, our families might not accept this. The clash of our backgrounds… it's tearing me apart.

Rasika: (teary-eyed) It's tearing me apart too, Mayank. I never imagined love could be so complicated.

In the quiet moments of conversations, we explored the contours of compromise and understanding. We recognized that love alone may not suffice to bridge the gap between our cultural backgrounds.

My eyes reflected the pain I felt.

Mayank: (voice breaking) I can't bear the thought of disappointing my parents, going against everything they believe in. But I can't imagine a life without you either.

Rasika: (softly) I never wanted to be the reason for your pain, Mayank. I love you too, but the reality of our situation is heart-breaking.

The cafe echoed with the sadness that lingered in our words, the harsh reality of societal expectations casting a long shadow over the love we cherished.

Mayank: (angrily) Why does society have to dictate our happiness? Why should we conform to these rigid norms?

Rasika: (resigned) I wish it were that simple, Mayank. But we can't ignore the fact that our families may never approve.

My frustration collided with the harsh truth, creating tension in the room.

Mayank: (frustrated) I thought love could conquer all, but it feels like we're fighting against an unyielding force.

Rasika: (teary-eyed) Love should be enough, shouldn't it? But reality is a cruel reminder of the battles we're up against.

The vulnerability in our voices laid bare the emotional toll of the crossroads we found ourselves standing at.

Mayank: (voice breaking) Maybe we're just not meant to be.

Rasika: (whispers) Don't say that, Mayank. I can't bear the thought of losing you.

My conflicted gaze met Rasika's, and in that moment, the place seemed to shrink around us, suffocating us with the harsh reality of circumstances.

Mayank: (regretful) I don't want to lose you either, but I can't ignore the turmoil this is causing. Maybe it's best if we face the inevitable and part ways.

Rasika: (heartbroken) Part ways? But... what about us?

Mayank: (voice breaking) Sometimes, love isn't enough. We have to accept the reality that surrounds us, even if it means breaking our own hearts.

The conversation was leaving towards a painful conclusion. The cafe, once filled with the promise of love, now echoed with the sorrow of an uncertain future and the heartbreaking realization that societal expectations had become humongous barriers to the love we had hoped would conquer all.

My gaze remained fixed on the floor, unable to meet the tear-filled eyes of Rasika, the pain etched on both our faces telling a story of heartbreak and resignation.

Rasika: (softly) I never thought it would come to this, Mayank. I believed in us.

Mayank: (whispers) So did I. But reality has a way of crushing our dreams.

Rasika: (teary-eyed) Are we really going to let go? Can't we fight against this, Mayank?

My internal struggle played out on my face as I grappled with the profound weight of our circumstances.

Mayank: (hesitates) I don't want to let you go, but I'm torn, torn between my love for you and the duty I feel towards my family.

Rasika: (pleading) Mayank, love should be our anchor. Can't we find a way to make it work?

Mayank: (resigned) I wish it were that simple. But the reality is that our families may never accept us, and I can't bear the thought of causing them pain.

Rasika: (desperate) Mayank, I can't imagine a life without you. Please, let's find a way. Let's fight for us.

My internal struggle reflected in my eyes, torn between the love I held for Rasika and the weight of familial expectations.

Mayank: (whispers) I don't want to lose you, but I also can't ignore the inevitable pain that awaits us. Maybe it's time to accept our reality.

Rasika: (voice breaking) So, this is it? We just let go?

Mayank: (regretful) I never wanted it to come to this, but I can't see a way forward. It's breaking my heart, too.

Rasika: (broken) If this is our reality, Mayank, I hope you find the happiness you deserve. I'll always cherish what we had.

Mayank: (choked up) You deserve the world, and I'm sorry we couldn't give that to each other.

As we sat in the cafe, love slipping through our fingers like grains of sand, the finality of our decision settled in. The harsh truth of societal expectations had claimed its toll where a love story, our love story, was not allowed to flourish. Even though I behaved like a matured guy all the while during our conversation, but when I realized that it will really mean living without her, I could not dare to take the decision.

"I can't live without you Rasika. I just Can't."

Those were my final words, and the last one-hour conversation of parting ways was all swept away. We decided that we will continue with the relationship and see how it goes. Since I had come to meet her in quick notice, I did not have much time and had to catch the train which leaves Jabapur at 3:30 PM. So, she quickly dropped me again to the railway station with a smile because we were going to continue together. Throughout the journey to Singrauli I was deeply lost in the thoughts and about the conversation that we had. Even though I did not have any answer about the cast issue, but I knew that this will not end here.

The Crash Landing

It was February 27th, 2015, tomorrow was my birthday and I wanted to gift myself something. It has been my habit that I give birthday gift to myself, and the habit has continued till today. It was year 2015 and after saving for almost two years I was going to buy a brand-new Honda Activa 125 cc. Since Nagri Niwas was a small village and there was no vehicle showroom, I had to go to Waidhan which was the main city area of Singrauli to buy my vehicle.

I along with Rai sir went to Waidhan by bus as in return we will have to drive the new vehicle back to Niwas. Before buying Activa, I did not know how to ride a two-wheeler. All I had ridden was bicycle that too of my cousins since we were too poor even to purchase a bicycle. My job certainly had changed our lifestyle and finally we could plan and buy something as expensive as an Activa.

So, once we were done with the payment, we started, and I asked Rai sir to drive first since I had no experience of riding. He drove it for good 50 KM then asked me to drive as we had to drive 50 more KM. Waidhan was 100 KM from Nagri Niwas and It shows how remote the location of Nagri Niwas village was. I started to drive, and it was not difficult. All I had to look after was accelerator and break as there are no gears or clutch in Activa. I was driving just fine and started loving it. As we were close to reaching Niwas, suddenly a cow came in running and mistakenly a new driver like me pressed the front brakes only and the vehicle was in good speed therefore it slipped and both of us fell from it. I was in a state of shock since it was the first day first ride of my new vehicle and I crashed it badly. I checked and saw a big scratch mark was at the front.

I was in a bad bad mood but fortunately both of us were safe and apart from that one scratch even the scooty was alright. Finally, it was around 7 in the evening when I reached Niwas. Even though we had a small accident, but I was still so glad to have finally purchased my new Honda Activa. I did not tell anyone, including my mother about the crash of the new activa.

The bustling streets of Nagri Niwas witnessed a new addition to the landscape as I proudly rode on my newly acquired Activa 125cc. The moment was not just a personal victory but a joyous occasion for the entire family, especially my mother and Nani.

My mother, with a warm smile, welcomed me as I parked the Activa in the courtyard. Her eyes gleamed with pride as she saw her son on his new vehicle, a symbol of progress and independence. Beside her, my nani, seated on a charpoy, observed the scene with a blend of curiosity and delight.

"Mayank, beta, this is such a wonderful surprise! Your new Activa looks splendid. How does it feel to ride it?" My mother inquired with genuine enthusiasm.

I couldn't contain my excitement, "It's amazing, Maa! The Activa is not just a vehicle; it's like a companion on the road. Smooth, efficient, and perfect for getting around the village. I can't believe I finally have my own scooter!"

My grandmother said, "In our times, we didn't have these fancy vehicles. Walking or cycling was the way to get around. But times have changed, and it's wonderful to see the convenience these new technologies bring."

Taking a moment to catch my breath, I continued, "You know, Maa, this Activa is not just for me. It's going to make my work in the village much more manageable. I can reach places faster, attend to banking needs efficiently, and, most importantly, serve the community better."

My mother nodded in agreement, "I've always admired your dedication to your work, Mayank. This Activa is not just a means of transport; it's a tool that will help you make a difference in the lives of the villagers. I'm proud of you, beta."

My grandmother added, "Back in my days, we would have to walk for miles to get anywhere. Having an Activa would have been a luxury! But times change, and it's heartening to see the progress and opportunities available for the younger generation."

The conversation continued, weaving through the threads of nostalgia, admiration, and a shared sense of accomplishment.

I felt a deep sense of gratitude for the support and understanding that my family, across generations, had always provided. The Activa, now a part of this familial narrative, carried with it the echoes of shared joys, dreams, and the enduring bond of our family.

Strings and Shutter

Despite the heavy workload and the challenges of my surroundings, I discovered two new passions in life: photography and playing the guitar.

I had recently purchased a DSLR camera, eager to explore the art of capturing moments through lenses. I had got Canon 750D back then and it was the most advanced DSLR camera which fit in my budget. Today having a DSLR is very common but back then, it surely was a luxary item since mobile phones did not have good enough cameras either.

Living in Nagri Niwas village, I was surrounded by breathtaking landscapes, rural cultures, and the simple beauty of everyday life. With my camera in hand, I went out to capture the essence of my surroundings.

From the golden hues of sunrise over the fields to the bustling rural market streets filled with colors and life, my lens captured it all. I found solace in framing moments frozen in time, allowing me to appreciate the beauty around me amidst the chaos of my daily routine.

Moreover, photography served as a form of expression for me. Through my lens, I told stories of resilience, hope, and the spirit of the people in my village. Each click of the shutter brought me closer to understanding the world around me and my place within it.

Despite my busy schedule, I found time to learn the guitar. With its soothing melodies and rhythmic tunes, the guitar became my companion in moments of solitude. It was Rasika who gifted me the guitar knowing I always wanted it.

In the quiet evenings after work, I used to a sit in a corner of my small room in Nagri Niwas, strumming the strings of my guitar. I lost myself in the music, letting the notes wash over me like gentle waves, calming my mind and rejuvenating my spirit. My favourite song to sing, listen and play was Aadat. My connection with "Adat" went beyond the surface; it became a companion that resonated with the nuances of my emotions. I have been listening to it since I was in class 12th, and I just fell in love with this song ever since I have heard it. The song accompanied me on long rides through the village on my Activa, providing a melodic backdrop to the changing scenes of rural life. Whether I found myself navigating the winding paths near the national tiger reserve (Sanjay Gandhi Tiger Reserve) or passing by the agricultural fields, "Adat" became a constant, weaving its melancholic magic into the fabric of my experiences.

Learning the guitar was a journey of patience and perseverance for me. Despite the initial challenges, I found joy in mastering new chords and melodies. With each practice session, I grew more confident in my abilities, finding fulfillment in the progress I made. Youtube played a significant role in my Guitar practice as there was no fomal class of Guitar in such a rural place.

What made my hobbies even more remarkable was the context in which I pursued them. Working in a remote village came with its own set of challenges – limited resources, erratic electricity, and long hours at the bank. However, I refused to let these obstacles dampen my spirits.

Instead, I saw my hobbies as a form of escape – a way to momentarily transcend the pressures of my daily life and connect with my passions. Whether I was out capturing the perfect shot or strumming my guitar under the starlit sky, I found joy in the simple pleasures that life had to offer.

In essence, my journey was a testament to the power of hobbies in bringing joy and fulfillment to our lives, even in the most challenging of circumstances. Through photography and music, I found solace, inspiration, and a sense of purpose amidst the chaos of my surroundings.

So, the next time you feel overwhelmed by the pressures of life, take a page out of my book. Find solace in the simple pleasures, pursue your passions with vigor, and let the joy of hobbies light up your world. After all, as I discovered, it's often the smallest moments that bring us the greatest happiness.

Sooooo Saaa Saiyaaaa

One of the difficulties with rural branches is that nobody wishes to work at such places and the branches are always understaffed. It was until a couple of years when bank finally posted two new clerks in our branch. One was Mr. Dileep Yadav who was from Seoni Distict of Madhya Pradesh and the other one was Manas Soni who belonged to Sagar, Madhya Pradesh. Just like me initially they were quite nervous to experience the huge number of customers who visited our branch in everyday banking. Manas was a decent and sweet guy who mingled with us quite well, while Dileep was a unique guy and his way of looking at the world was quite different from others. Initially we were not really fond of him as his work was not perfect and he made several mistakes. He was made the head cashier of the branch since he joined before Manas and was senior by a day. Every cashier has to keep the keys of the cash vault.

Cash counter was the busiest counter of the whole branch since ours was a payment branch and people mostly came here to withdraw money which was credited in their accounts either by the government or from the power plant.

Soon, both of them were settled in the style this branch was working with and also the rural life of Nagri Niwas. Manas was working at the miscellaneous request counter, same as what I was doing while working in SBB Barhi Branch. He was good at his work and soon picked up the pace. Both of them were hard wrking but Dileep was unique in his approach. He was also one of the funniest guys that I had ever met in my life before. One incident I still remember when branch was completely filled with customers, and it was a hot day in Singrauli. There was a long line infront of cash counter and it was just getting longer with each passing minute. Cash counter is a closed cabin, and the temperature gets hotter than the most parts of the branch since maximum customers gather around it. Meena sir was busy with customer queries, Rai sir was passing cash deposit and transfer cheque vouchers, I was opening savings accounts, Manas was posting cheques and printing passbooks, and Dileep was receiving cash and was also making payments.

Out of nowhere, suddenly Dileep stood up while there were more than a hundred customers inside the branch, and he started looking at them with a serious look. Customers in rural area are usually very simple and they were afraid to see him stading, expecting him to shout at them for making too much noise or not following the line discipline. Dileep started shouting,

"Sooooo saaa Saiyaaaa Saiyaaaaaa Sasaaang Sasaaang"

"Sooooo saaa Saiyaaaa Saiyaaaaaa Sasaaang Sasaaang"

It was a strange sound and he kept on repeating it. Poor customers were in shock seeing him do that. They were unable to come to an answer why Cashier Sahab was making that strange sound. Well, nobody had any answer, but we all were laughing hard. Soon he stopped doing it and called the next customer for payment. This was just one of the funny things which Dileep used to do, and we mostly had no clue why he did this, but we enjoyed it. Soon soo saaaa saiyaaaan saiyaaaaaan sasang sasang became our theme. After this incident, we asked him the actual meaning of this song which he never answered.

Another day Dileep was sitting in the cash counter. While I was passing the payment vouchers. During the busiest hours of our branch banking a beautiful lady came to Dileep's counter. It was a rare sight to find a beautiful woman like her in our branch. In urban branches, there are several lady customers and a good number of them are pretty. Since it was a very busy day and more than usual number of customers were there inside the branch for payment, even Manas was making payments. So, Dileep in the backside of the voucher of that lady, wrote a message for me. "Mayank

Sir, please send the lady to me and not Mridul after you pass her voucher."

I was stunned to see the message and was even laughing at his act. After the voucher was passed, the lady who was in the line in front of Manas was called by Dileep for her payment. She was quite confused as initially her line was different. Dileep made her stand in front of his counter for more than two hours. He kept looking at her and was making regular conversation with her but was not paying her. Even the lady was smiling as a government bank employee was taking interest in her. Both were talking and all other staff, including the customers were noticing their conversation. It was about 4 PM when Dileep finally gave her the payment. He gave her his phone number along with cash payment and finally she left the branch. This was another incident of him doing something which was not expected from him. Such was Dileep.

Dinner with the Sarpanch

Our bank was the only government institute in the area and therefore we were given so much respect by the locals. This is not experienced in cities or other urban areas. Nagri Niwas village was quite backward when it comes to caste system. Being a Brahmin helped me a lot, though personally I do not endorse this system. One day after a hectic branch day, we were invited by Sarpanch and Secretary of the village for dinner. The dinner party offered a unique setting for interaction between the village head and the bank staff. Such parties were not new and bank staff was often invited, but this was the first time when our batch staff was going in such a party together. The event unfolded in a manner that reflected both the cultural richness of the region and the surprise of the bank staff at the unexpected hospitality in a remote part of India. While we were invited, I initially thought it will be a rural party with local drinks and foods having limited resources.

When we reached there, we saw numeros mouth watering dishes were waiting for us. There were fresh fish, Desi chicken, and other local dishes as well.

The Sarpanch had a huge piece of land right next to the river, where the party was set up. We sat down in a nice green area and felt really welcomed. The Sarpanch, who was well-respected in the village, greeted us warmly. He shared stories about the village and its history, which made us feel connected to the place.

Just as the starters were served, we were astonished to see three bottles of Black Label. Such a premium whisky was offered to us which was not expected in a rural setting.

The land by the river was huge and showed how hard the villagers worked to make a living. They grew crops and took care of the land, showing their strong connection to nature.

The food was simple but delicious. Each dish reminded us of the old times and the traditions passed down through generations. We enjoyed the flavors and felt grateful for the chance to experience village life.

More than just a meal, the party was about coming together as a community. It reminded us of the importance of staying connected to our roots and cherishing our shared values. The sarpanch, proud of the local dishes, explained the significance of each item served. Initially surprised by the gastronomic excellence in such a remote village, we gradually engaged in conversations about the ingredients, cooking methods, and the cultural symbolism associated with the food.

Amidst the flavorful dishes and the exchange of culture, the sarpanch also discussed the challenges faced by the village in terms of infrastructure, education, and healthcare.

As the evening progressed and the cold night enveloped Nagri Niwas, we found ourselves not only enjoying the warmth of the hospitality but also gaining a deeper understanding of the community they served. The sarpanch, in turn, appreciated the genuine interest shown by us in the village's affairs. The dialogue that unfolded during the dinner party laid the foundation for future collaborations and partnerships, emphasizing the potential for synergy between the financial institutions and rural communities.

It was getting late and we started feeling sleepy as we had arrived after a hectic day at bank, so we requested Sahu Ji to permit us to leave. He had sent his own vehicle to pick us up from our room and he dropped us home as well. Altogether, it was a nice evening at Sarpanch's house, and we thoroughly enjoyed it.

Bahar Nikal

It was my third year working in Nagri Niwas branch in January 2016 and most customers were known to me by face. All bankers will agree that there are a few customers who consider themselves VIP and want all their works to be given priority over others even if it is not ethical or legally correct. Even though I was still very young, but I had learnt to deal with such customers and somehow managed to handle them smartly. There was this guy named Dheerendra Tripathi who was known for his notorious and bossy nature who was also a customer of our branch. His father was a patwari in nearby village and being patwari was a big thing in Niwas and therefore, he was well known by the villagers.

One fine day Dheerendra came to my counter for payment of a cheque and Meena sir was on leave therefore, I was clearing the cheques. He had brought cheque of his father's account for cash payment and once cashier entered the cheque into the system for payment, it came to me for verification. I entered the financial transaction number written on the cheque and opened the signature. I could see that signature on Cheque before me did not match with the signatures submitted in bank records of that account. I looked at it carefully knowing Dheerendra will not like it if I returned the cheque. Making payment of such a cheque where the signature is mismatched may have legal issues in future and therefore, I could not clear it anyhow.

"Signature is not matching with the bank records Dheerendra."

I looked at him and informed about the mismatch.

"Sir it's my father's signature only. I come here regularly, and everyone knows me you can ask them."

He replied in his usual arrogant tone.

"Sorry brother but I cannot make payment since signature is not matching. Please get it re-signed or you may call your father to sign it again."

I politely asked him.

"What do you mean to call him here. Like he is free just for your cheque payment. You can not stop me from withdrawing my own money."

Dheerendra was furious.

"It is none of my business to get into anyone's personal details, but it is not your account but your father's account from which you are trying to withdraw money. I am sorry but I cannot pass this cheque."

I was now irritated with his attitude.

"Aisa hai sahib ap bahar miliye apko niyam kayda batate hain ham."

He threatened me openly to come out.

He thought that threatening me will have his cheque cleared but it had just opposite effect on me and I lost all my calmness and stood up.

"Let's settle it right now, let us go out. What are you going to teach me?"

I stood up leaving all my vouchers on the desk and asked him to come out. He did not expect this kind of reaction from me and hesitantly followed me.

There were more than 100 customers inside the branch, and more were standing outside waiting for their turn to come. Seeing me coming out like that was something they had never witnessed and actually this side of mine was also new to me. I am normally a very cool and calm guy who uses his brain, but I do not know what triggered me that day and I took such a dangerous step. It was his village, and I was surrounded by his people all around me, yet I dared to challenge him for such a confrontation.

"What I am asking is lawfully correct and I want you to call your father right now and tell him that I am not allowing you to withdraw money from his account because the signature is not matching with the bank records. In future if someday he arrives and lodges a complaint that he did not issue this cheque then who will take the responsibility of unauthorised withdrawal?"

Somehwere I had this doubt that he was withdrawing money from his father's account using forged signature and his father did not have any idea about it.

"If today I allow you to withdraw money from your father's account while the signature is not matching, then it will become a practice, and anyone will start withdrawing money from anyone's account."

People around me noded in agreement.

When I asked him to call his father his face turned red, and he was not in position to reply. He did not say anything and just listened to me. I was shivering in anger and was literally shouting at him.

"I will lodge an official police complaint against you for creating hurdle in government institute's daily operation."

I threatened him back and I was now liking this whole situation. He was taken back by my response and just listened to me silently. Then my branch head along with other customers who were known to me, and other staff came out where all this drama was going on. They tried to calm me down and I returned his cheque which he kept with him without any further question.

After this incident Dheerendra never confronted me and started respecting me. I learnt a lesson that sometimes it is important to take bold step and bravery has its own rewards.

Stone Pelting

The sun hung low in the sky as I embarked on my journey from Singrauli to Rewa District, a sense of anticipation coursing through my veins. I had been nominated for a seven-day training on bank products in Bhopal, and the prospect of expanding my knowledge filled me with excitement.

Boarding the first bus from Singrauli to Sidhi District, I settled into my seat, eager to reach my destination. The journey was uneventful, as the bus was in a very poor condition and was completely packed with villagers.

Arriving in Sidhi, I switched buses, the anticipation of the training was in my mind. Little did I know, the next leg of my journey would be fraught with danger and uncertainty. Since the weather of Sidhi was no different than that of Singrauli, therefore I ordered a fresh juice and as I was having it, immediately I was taken back in time to the day when Ankush offered me juice at the first day of my stay at SBTC.

As the bus rumbled through the countryside, the landscape gradually shifted, the familiar sights of Singrauli giving way to the rugged terrain of Sidhi district.

The district of Sidhi was known for its predominantly Thakur population, a fact that held little significance for me until that moment. But as the bus was in its way through the narrow roads of Chorhat, where the Thakurs held sway, I felt a knot form in the pit of my stomach.

Suddenly, without warning, chaos erupted around us as stones rained down upon the bus with alarming ferocity. Panic seized hold of the passengers, their cries of fear mingling with the sound of shattering glass as the rain of stones got stronger.

In that moment, fear gripped me badly, paralyzing me as I huddled in my seat, praying for safety amidst the chaos. The bus driver, a Brahman by birth, maneuvered skillfully through the onslaught, his determination unwavering in the face of adversity.

As the minutes stretched into eternity, the stone pelting finally stopped, leaving behind a trail of destruction and devastation in its wake. Surveying the damage, I felt a surge of gratitude wash over me, a sense of relief at having emerged unhurt from the incident.

The fact that the bus, owned by a Brahman, had become the target of Thakur aggression spoke volumes about the deep-seated animosity that pervaded the region.

As the dust settled and the echoes of the attack faded into the distance, a tense silence descended upon the bus.

Passengers exchanged worried glances, their faces expressing mixture of fear and disbelief at the sudden onslaught they had endured.

Gathering our wits, we began to cautiously assess the extent of the damage, our hands trembling as we surveyed the shattered remnants of windows and the dents on the once pristine exterior of the bus. It was a reminder of the fragility of life, of how quickly peace could be shattered by the whims of violence and hatred.

Amidst the chaos, conversation began to ripple through the crowd, tentative voices seeking solace and reassurance amidst the turmoil. Some exchanged nervous laughter, their attempts to lighten the mood falling flat in the face of the gravity of the situation.

"It's madness," someone muttered, their voice tinged with disbelief. "What could possibly drive people to such senseless violence?"

Others nodded in agreement as they grappled with the implications of the attack. For many, it was their first experience of such attack, a stark wake-up call to the harsh realities of the world beyond the safety of their own communities.

As the initial shock began to fade, whispers of speculation filled the air, each passenger offering their own theories as to the motives behind the attack. Some blamed long-standing rivalries between Thakurs and Brahmins, while others pointed fingers at political unrest simmering beneath the surface.

In the blink of an eye, our journey had been derailed by forces beyond our control, leaving us stranded in a sea of uncertainty and fear.

And so, with hearts heavy but spirits unbroken, we pressed on towards our destination. Though the scars of the attack would remain long after the physical wounds had healed, we refused to let fear dictate our path forward.

As we continued our journey towards Rewa District, the weight of the incident hung heavy in the air, casting a shadow over the once vibrant landscape. The stark contrast between the Thakur-dominated Sidhi district and the predominantly Brahman stronghold of Rewa served as a reminder of the deep-rooted divisions that plagued our society.

Arriving in Rewa, I couldn't shake the sense of unease that lingered within me, a lingering reminder of the fragility of peace in a world fraught with conflict and strife. Yet, amidst the chaos and uncertainty, a glimmer of hope emerged, a belief that through understanding and empathy, we could bridge the chasm that divided us and forge a path towards unity and reconciliation.

Kare Koi Bhare Koi

In the sleepy village of Niwas despite the rustic charm of the village, one aspect of rural life proved to be a constant source of frustration: the lack of convenient transportation options.

Even though Niwas was connected to railway line and was having a railway station, but its status as a stop for only slow passenger trains left much to be desired. Express trains breezed past it mocking on us as they travelled towards destinations unknown.

It was on one fateful day when an unexpected turn of events led to a huge trouble for our branch manager Mr. Manoj Sharma. My branch manager was fron Jaunpur Uttar Pradesh and he was travelling in an express train to reach niwas. The scheduled stop of his train was not niwas as it was supposed to stop at the next stop Sarai which was 50 kilometer away from Niwas.

As the express train hurtled towards its scheduled stop at Sarai, fate intervened in the form of our mischievous washerman, Dhaniram. With a flick of his wrist, he pulled the emergency brake chains, bringing the train to an abrupt halt at the Niwas station.

My branch manager was travelling in the AC coach and was not aware about the situation. He knew that train was scheduled to stop at Sarai station and then he was to take local conveyance from Sarai to Niwas. As he witnessed the train stopping at Niwas station, he considered it to be an opportunity too good to let go. He stepped off the train, blissfully unaware of the chaos that awaited him. For the regular updowners it is a known fact that railway police start searching for the culprits who illegaly stop the train using emergency breaks. Dhaniram the washer who originally had pulled the chain was accustomed to this and was waiting for the police to go and once the train was ready to move only then he would get off the train. When he saw the branch manager disembarking from the train, he tried to stop him.

Shouting warnings from the gate in the general coach, he hoped to prevent disaster and spare our unsuspecting manager from the clutches of authority. All his efforts were in vain, as my branch manager, unaware of the situation, descended from the train and into the waiting arms of the railway police. To his shock, he found himself accused of the heinous crime of illegal chain pulling, a crime he had not committed.

Desperate to clear his name, my branch manager protested his innocence to the railway police, but to no avail. Reports had already been filed, and the wheels of justice were set in motion, albeit in the wrong direction.

Police Officer: Well, well, well, who do we have here? A government bank manager caught red-handed pulling the emergency brake chain?

Branch Manager: (sputtering) No, officer, you've got it all wrong! I didn't pull the chain; it was a misunderstanding!

Police Officer: Oh, sure, and I suppose the train just decided to stop at Niwas station all on its own, did it?

Branch Manager: (frantically) No, no, you see, it was our washerman, Dhaniram! I do not know why in the world did he do it. I only came out because I thought train has stopped here because of no signal.

Police Officer: (raising an eyebrow) And why would your washerman want to do something like that?

Branch Manager: (sheepishly) He's a bit of a joker, officer. Always looking for ways to stir up trouble. I swear! Please, you have to believe me!

Police Officer: (sighing) Look, I've heard a lot of excuses in my time, but this one takes the cake. You're coming with me to Sarai, and we'll let the higher-ups' sort this mess out.

Branch Manager: (defeated) But officer, I'm innocent! I demand a fair trial!

Police Officer: (rolling his eyes) Save it for the judge. Let's go.

As the branch manager was escorted away in handcuffs, he couldn't help but wonder how he had ended up in such a pitiful situation. Little did he know, his misadventures were only just beginning, and the road ahead would be filled with twists and turns that even the most seasoned banker couldn't have predicted.

With a heavy heart, my branch manager was escorted to Sarai, where he faced the daunting prospect of explaining his actions to local authorities. However, fate smiled upon him as he found allies in the form of local MLA and influential figures, who intervened on his behalf and secured his release. As ours was the only bank in the nearby villages, most influential personalities including the local MLA were having their accounts in our branch and therefore we knew them.

Witnessing the whole drama, Dhaniram travelled in the same train and followed my branch manager and met him in the Railway Police Office in Sarai.

Manager: Dhaniram, what in the world were you thinking, pulling that emergency brake chain?!

Dhaniram: Sir, I-I-I'm sorry! I didn't mean for all this to happen!

Manager: Sorry doesn't solve it, Dhaniram! Do you have any idea what you've done? I was almost arrested!

Dhaniram: I know, I know! It was so stupid of me. I never thought they'd actually catch you!

Manager: Well, they did, and now I've been accused of illegal chain pulling! Do you have any idea how embarrassing that is?

Dhaniram: I swear, sir, I didn't mean for any of this to happen. I have been doing it from long but never got caught.

Manager: This is a disaster, Dhaniram! I could have ended up in jail!

Dhaniram: I'm really sorry, sir. Is there anything I can do to make it up to you?

Manager: I don't know, Dhaniram. I don't know if there's anything you can do to undo the chaos you've caused.

Dhaniram: Please, sir, give me a chance to make things right. I'll do anything!

Manager: Anything, you say? Well, there is one thing you could do…

Dhaniram: Anything, sir! Just name it!

Manager: I need someone to take the fall for this mess. Someone willing to go to court and pretend to be the one who pulled the chain.

Dhaniram: You want me to take the blame?

Manager: Yes, Dhaniram. I need you to step up and be the sacrificial lamb.

Dhaniram: But sir, won't that mean I'll get in trouble?

Manager: Possibly, but I'll make sure you're taken care of. You'll be compensated for your troubles.

Dhaniram: Well, I suppose if it means helping you out, I'll do it.

Manager: Thank you, Dhaniram. I appreciate your willingness to take responsibility for your actions.

Dhaniram: Don't mention it, sir. I just hope this all blows over soon.

Manager: Me too, Dhaniram. Me too.

Dhaniram, the true culprit behind the chaos, was approached and compensated to stand in as a scapegoat for my branch manager. With a mixture of guilt and amusement, he found himself thrust into the spotlight.

As the dust settled and the village returned to its usual tranquility, the incident served as a cautionary tale, a reminder of the unpredictable nature of rural life and the importance of vigilance in the face of mischief. And though laughter echoed through the streets of Niwas as the tale was retold time and time again, the memory of that fateful day lingered as a testament to the quirks and eccentricities of village life.

Chapter VIII

My First Transfer

The following evening after a usual tiring day at work, I found myself once again immersed in the soothing rhythm of my nightly call with Rasika. This time, however, the conversation took a different turn as we began discussing our shared dreams for the future.

"Mayank, what do you envision when you think about us living together in Jabalpur?" Rasika asked, her curiosity laced with anticipation.

I leaned back, a smile playing on my lips, "I picture lazy Sunday mornings, exploring the city hand in hand, finding hidden gems in the chaos. Maybe we'll have our favorite spot for chai, where we can just sit and watch the world go by."

Rasika chuckled, "That sounds perfect. And what about our evenings?"

"I imagine cooking together, or at least attempting to," I replied with a laugh. "And then cozying up on the couch, binge-watching our favorite shows. Simple moments that become the highlights of our day. Then our nights will be wilder than ever before."

Our conversation painted a vivid picture of a life with shared experiences and the beauty of the ordinary. The dreams we wove together that night created a vision for a future we both longed to embrace.

As the weeks unfolded, the anticipation of my move to Jabalpur grew, each passing day a countdown to the moment we could bridge the physical distance that still separated us. The job transfer was progressing, and the prospect of sharing a city was now more tangible than ever.

One evening, a call took an unexpected turn when Rasika shared,

"Mayank, I've been thinking. Once you're here, why don't we take a trip somewhere? Just the two of us, a mini getaway."

The idea sparked excitement in my eyes, "That sounds amazing! Any particular place in mind?"

Rasika paused, her voice tinged with mischief, "How about Goa? Somewhere away from the hustle, where we can just be together, away from work and city chaos."

The notion of a secluded retreat resonated within me, and we began planning the details of our proposed escape to beaches. The mere thought of shared adventures and quiet moments nestled in nature brought a renewed sense of joy to our connection.

As the day of my potential transfer approached, the anticipation rose. Late-night calls reminded us that our love story was evolving and soon we will be living together in Jabalpur.

Finally, the news arrived—but my transfer to Jabalpur was not approved, rather I was transferred to Satna, another district of Madhya Pradesh. My relocation was planned but Satna was not the city I wanted to work in. Our long-awaited cohabitation and a shared vision of building a home together had to wait for some more time.

The night before my move, emotions ran high. "Can you believe it, Rasika? Tomorrow, I'll be in Satna, I really wanted to be transferred to Jabalpur yar," I expressed, a mix of sadness and frustration in my voice.

Rasika's response was a soft reassurance, "I can't wait to have you here, Mayank. I also wanted you to be transferred to Jabalpur. I really miss you."

As we said our goodnights, the dream of waking up in the same city, breathing the same air, and sharing the extraordinary moments together, was broken.

The sun rose on a new day, marking the beginning of my work at Satna. I was going to miss all my staff and customers of Nagri Niwas. It was my first branch and though it was a really difficult posting, but it will remain closest to my heart forever. I will consider it my good behaviour and service that even customers were extremely sad to know about my transfer. But such is the job of working as an officer in a government bank, you got to keep moving.

Jealousy and Phone Hack

The news of my transfer from Singrauli to Satna brought with it a blend of excitement and anticipation. I arrived in Satna in June 2016, a town in Madhya Pradesh known for its historical significance and cement plants, I couldn't help but feel a mix of nervousness and eagerness about the new chapter that awaited me. In comparison to Singrauli, Satna was way better as far as branch and city was concerned. It was only 100 KM from my hometown Katni, and the branch was in urban area and was also very well connected. The building was also new with all the modern amenities since it was opened only a couple of years ago.

My first day at the Satna branch was all about introductions with unfamiliar faces. Carrying the weight of my experience from Singrauli, I approached the team with an open mind. The banking landscape may change, I thought, but the essence of building relationships and importance of teamwork remains constant.

The branch manager, Mr. Pandey, welcomed me with a warm smile. "Mayank, we're thrilled to have you here. Satna has its own rhythm, and I'm confident you'll find your place in the symphony of our operations."

A team of seasoned bankers and fresh faces greeted me with a mixture of curiosity and camaraderie. Rajesh, the loan officer who was a local, shared stories of the town's rich history, underscoring the cultural tapestry that defined Satna. Anjali, the branch's customer service representative, offered insights into the community's dynamics and the unique financial needs that shaped our interactions.

As I settled into my new role, I found myself collaborating with colleagues well. The town presented its own set of challenges and opportunities, required me to adapt my expertise according to the local landscape. After spending a month in the branch, I matched with the pace and understood the culture in which the banking services were offered in Satna.

Among my colleagues at the branch, Rajesh was a kind-hearted soul who happened to be handicapped. He was entrusted with the responsibility of maintaining our ATM. One day he, inadvertently loaded a stack of 500-rupee notes into the tray designated for 100-rupee bills. It was a simple error, one that could have happened to anyone, yet its repercussions would be felt far and wide.

The following day brought an unexpected turn of events when our branch manager received a distressing call from a customer. The ATM machine, it seemed, was dispensing more money than what was being withdrawn. Panic rippled through the staff as we grappled with the implications of such a discovery. How could this have happened? What would be the consequences?

Rajesh bore the brunt of the situation, his mistake casting a shadow of doubt over his competence and integrity. He was scolded harshly, his reputation tarnished in the eyes of colleagues and superiors alike. As an inquiry was launched to ascertain the extent of the error and its financial implications, tensions ran high, and the atmosphere within the branch grew strained.

Recognizing the gravity of the situation, I took it upon myself to assist Rajesh in rectifying his mistake. With meticulous attention to detail, we combed through transaction records and CCTV footage, piecing together the puzzle of the excess money dispensed by the ATM.

The task was daunting, fraught with challenges and setbacks, yet we persevered, driven by a shared commitment to righting the wrongs of the past. Together, we traced every transaction linked to the erroneous dispensation, meticulously documenting each step of our journey towards restitution.

Through our combined efforts, we were able to recover a significant portion of the excess funds, totaling 1,20,000 rupees. It was a small victory in the face of adversity, but tracing ATM card holders of other banks was a tough task.

Yet, even as we celebrated our success, there remained a lingering sense of unfinished business. A sum of 70,000 rupees was still left to be recovered, a reminder of the debt owed to the bank and its customers. With a heavy heart, Rajesh took it upon himself to bear the burden of his mistake, offering to compensate for the remaining amount from his own pocket.

His gesture of accountability spoke volumes about his character, serving as a beacon of hope in a time of uncertainty. In a world where trust is often elusive, Rajesh's willingness to take responsibility for his actions stood as a shining example of integrity and honor.

As the dust settled and everything was normal in the branch, we emerged stronger and more united than ever before.

Rajesh had a close friend named Namita, whose radiant beauty was only surpassed by her warm personality.

It was on one fateful day when Namita first crossed paths with me at the bank. Our eyes met, and in that moment, I felt a spark ignite within me. She was undeniably stunning, her presence commanding attention wherever she went. Little did I know, our brief encounter would set into motion a series of events that would test the very fabric of my character. In the days that followed, Namita added me on Facebook, and soon, we found ourselves engrossed in conversations that stretched late into the night. Our chats were laced with laughter and shared interests, and with each passing day, I found myself drawn to her magnetic charm.

However, amidst the blossoming connection between Namita and me, I couldn't shake the feeling of guilt at the corners of my conscience. You see, I was acutely aware of Rajesh's feelings for Namita, and I couldn't bear the thought of betraying his trust. Driven by a sense of duty and loyalty, I made the difficult decision to confide in Rajesh about Namita's growing fondness for me. I hoped that by being transparent about the situation, I could prevent any potential heartache or misunderstanding. Little did I know, my well-intentioned actions would set off a chain reaction of betrayal and deceit.

Rajesh, consumed by jealousy and fueled by misguided intentions, misconstrued my honesty as an act of betrayal. In his eyes, I was perceived as a threat, a rival who was trying to steal the woman he held dear. Blinded by his emotions, Rajesh took the help of a friend who worked in the IT sector to create a devious plan of retaliation.

Before I knew it, my world came crashing down around me as I became the unwitting victim of a malicious scheme. My mobile phone, once a lifeline of communication, became a tool of manipulation in their hands to tarnish my reputation. They hacked into my device, assuming my identity to place deceitful calls to Namita and her relatives. The malicious ploy didn't stop there; they even sent a letter filled with derogatory remarks, all under the guise of my name. Initially I was not aware of what was happening with me but later on I realized it was Rajesh. How could those whom I considered friends stoop so low? How could they betray the very bonds of trust that held our camaraderie together? I was clueless about everything and was afraid that any given day police will catch me.

It was a long and arduous journey, one fraught with pain and heartache, but with each passing day, I found solace in the knowledge that adversity only served to strengthen my resolve.

One day the ringing of the phone pierced through the silence of my mind, bringing me back to the harsh reality of the situation. With a heavy heart, I picked up the receiver, bracing myself for the storm that was about to descend upon me.

"Hello?" I answered tentatively, my voice barely above a whisper.

The voice on the other end was filled with emotion of anger and despair. It was Namita's mother, her words a full of accusations and threats that cut through me like a knife.

"How could you do this to my daughter?" she demanded, her voice trembling with barely contained rage. "Do you realize the pain you've caused her? She's talking about ending her life because of you!"

My heart plummeted like a stone in my chest, the weight of her words crushing me beneath their unbearable burden. I struggled to find the words to defend myself, to convey the truth amidst the accusations.

"Mrs. Gupta, please, you have to believe me," I pleaded, the desperation evident in my voice. "I swear, I had nothing to do with any of this. I would never do anything to hurt Namita."

But my protests fell on deaf ears, drowned out by the tide of anguish and despair that threatened to engulf us both. Mrs. Gupta's grief was palpable, her pain a tangible presence that hung heavy in the air between us.

"You expect me to believe that?" she scoffed; her tone was filled with bitter disbelief. "My daughter is in tears because of you, and you have the audacity to deny your involvement?"

Tears pricked at the corners of my eyes, a silent testament to the agony that gripped my soul. How could I make her understand, make her see that I was as much a victim in all of this as Namita herself?

"I know how this looks, Mrs. Gupta, but I swear to you, I am telling the truth," I implored, my voice cracking with emotion. "I would never do anything to hurt Namita. Please, you have to believe me."

But belief was a fragile thing, easily shattered by the weight of suspicion and mistrust. Despite my earnest pleas, Mrs. Gupta didn't believe me, her resolve unyielding in the face of my protests.

"I don't want to hear any more excuses," she declared. "If anything happens to my daughter because of you, I will hold you personally responsible."

With a heavy heart, I listened as the line went dead, the echoes of Mrs. Gupta's accusations reverberating in my ears long after the conversation had ended. In that moment, I felt utterly powerless, a pawn in a game of betrayal and deceit that threatened to consume us all.

As I sat alone in the suffocating silence of my despair, I prayed for a resolution, for a glimmer of hope amidst the darkness that threatened to engulf me whole. But deep down, I knew that the road ahead would be fraught with uncertainty and hardship, a journey paved with the shattered fragments of trust and innocence lost.

From Shadows to Light

As I grappled with the turmoil of betrayal and deceit of recent events, an unexpected ray of hope emerged in the form of my childhood friend, Ashraf. Towering and formidable, Ashraf was a bodybuilder with a gentle heart and a keen intellect.

One fine day the streets of Satna buzzed with activity as I received an unexpected call. It was Ashraf, a name etched in the corridors of my childhood memories. The excitement in Ashraf's voice was visible through the phone, triggering a flood of nostalgia and anticipation. We agreed to meet at a cafe in the heart of Satna—a place where the echoes of old friendships could mingle with the present.

As I entered the cafe, the aroma of freshly brewed coffee mingled with the anticipation of remembering a bond that time had gently tucked away. The door opened, and in walked Ashraf, a familiar face whom I remember since my childhood. The two childhood friends, now adults with responsibilities and experiences shaping our lives, shared a moment of recognition and joy.

"Mayank!" Ashraf exclaimed, his eyes lighting up with a mix of surprise and delight. "I can't believe you're here in Satna. It's been ages!"

My face broke into a smile as I embraced Ashraf warmly. "Ashraf, bro, it's truly a pleasant surprise. Satna has its own rhythm, and it seems fate has brought us together again."

As I poured out my heart to him, detailing the events that had led me to the brink of despair, his shock mirrored my own.

"I can't believe Rajesh would do something like this even after the kind of support you gave him with the ATM transactions," he muttered with disbelief. "But we can't let him get away with it."

At first, our thoughts turned to vengeance, a desire to make him pay for he had wronged me. But as we weighed the consequences of such actions, a different course of action began to take shape in our minds.

"We need to confront Namita and her mother," Ashraf declared, his voice resolute with determination. "They deserve to know the truth, and we owe it to ourselves to set things right."

I nodded in agreement, a ray of hope igniting within me at the prospect of reclaiming my innocence and clearing my name. Together, Ashraf and I made a plan to bring the harsh reality of the situation to light, to unveil the lie that had dragged my life into the darkness.

The following day, armed with resolve and determination, we set out to confront Namita and her mother. With measured steps and a steely resolve, we approached their home, the weight of anticipation hanging heavy in the air.

"Mrs. Gupta, Namita, please," I began, my voice steady despite the turmoil raging within. "I need you to hear me out. There's been a misunderstanding, and I need to set the record straight."

Their expressions softened slightly; curiosity met with skepticism as they listened to my words. With Ashraf's unwavering support at my side, I recounted the events that had transpired, laying bare the truth of the situation for all to see.

To their credit, Namita and her mother listened with open-mindedness, their initial skepticism giving way to a realization of the depth of deceit that had been perpetrated against me. As the pieces of the puzzle fell into place, the truth emerged with clarity amidst the fog of uncertainty.

"I had no idea," Namita whispered, her voice tinged with regret. "I'm so sorry, I never meant for any of this to happen."

Tears welled in Mrs. Gupta's eyes as she reached out to me, a silent gesture of reconciliation amidst the mistrust and betrayal. In that moment, I felt a glimmer of hope stir within me, a renewed sense of purpose born from the ashes of despair.

With the truth laid bare before us, Ashraf and I left Namita and her mother to grapple with actual situation. Though the road ahead remained uncertain, I took solace in the knowledge that I was no longer alone in my struggle, that with Ashraf's steadfast support by my side, I could face whatever challenges lay ahead with courage and resilience.

Sun, Sand and Serenity

I and Rasika were planning for our trip to Goa from a long time. Our much-anticipated trip to Goa unfolded like a dream, with the sun-kissed beaches, vibrant markets, and the amazing rhythm of the coastal state.

The moment our plane touched down in Goa, the air carried the promise of adventure. The aroma of sea salt and coconut lingered in the air as we stepped into the warm embrace of the coastal breeze.

The first day was dedicated to the beaches. We visited Palolem, where golden sands met the gentle waves. With the sun overhead, I and Rasika walked along the shoreline, our footsteps leaving imprints that whispered tales of love and exploration.

In the vibrant energy of the flea market, we saw a mix of handmade crafts, vibrant clothing, and unique trinkets. Hand in hand, we went through the stalls, choosing souvenirs that would serve as reminders of our Goan vacation.

Evenings in Goa were synonymous with lively beach shacks and the soft glow of fairy lights. Soon we were immersed in the music of the coastal night, we enjoyed delicious seafood, exchanging laughter and stories under the open sky. The rhythmic beat of the ocean waves became the backdrop to our conversations, creating an ambiance that seemed to have paused time.

The second day started with the promise of exploration. We went to explore the historic charm of Old Goa, where centuries-old churches and cathedrals stood as testaments to the region's rich heritage. The detailed architecture and serene ambiance provided a stark contrast to the lively beaches of Goa.

The trip wouldn't be complete without a taste of adventure. The third day we enjoyed the thrill of water sports at Calangute Beach. Parasailing allowed us to soar above the coastline, the panoramic view of the Arabian Sea spreading out beneath us. The adrenaline rush was at its peak as we sailed on a banana boat, the sea breeze tousling our hair.

Evenings in Goa were a celebration of nightlife, and Baga Beach with its vibrant clubs and beachside party was the best place for us. We danced under the moonlit sky amidst the lively crowd, the rhythm of the music merging with the crashing waves. Goa's nightlife became a canvas for the spontaneity of our love, painted with the colors of celebration. First three days were scheduled to roam around each and every corner of Goa and after that we had couple of more days just to relax and enjoy the goan vibes.

Under the enchanting Goan sky, with the rhythmic waves of the Arabian Sea as our companion, we found ourselves on the golden sands of Anjuna Beach. As we settled on a blanket spread beneath a beautiful palm tree, the air was filled with the intoxicating scent of sea salt and the promise of an evening full of love.

As we indulged in the beautiful sunset infront of us, our conversation danced between memories and dreams.

"Remember the first time we spoke about our dreams?" I said, my gaze fixed on the horizon.

Rasika nodded, her eyes reflecting the hues of the setting sun. "It feels like a lifetime ago, yet here we are, living some of those dreams together."

Conversation was all about our journey till today– the late-night calls, the challenges of distance, and the shared triumphs. The evening unfolded as a canvas where words painted emotions as we sat against the timeless backdrop of the beach.

As twilight enveloped Anjuna, I took a moment to gaze into Rasika's eyes, the fading sunlight casting a soft glow on her face. "Rasika, do you ever wonder about the magic of this moment? Here we are, on Anjuna Beach, sharing dreams and creating memories. It's like a scene from a movie, yet it's our reality."

Rasika smiled, her hand finding its way to me. "Life has a way of surprising us, doesn't it? And I wouldn't have it any other way. This, right here, feels like a chapter from our own love story."

We fell into a comfortable silence, the ebb and flow of the tide becoming a backdrop to the unspoken connection between us. With the stars beginning to twinkle overhead, I reached into the bag, revealing a small diary.

"I thought we could write down our wishes for the future," I suggested, handing Rasika a pen.

The diary exchanged hands between us, becoming a vessel for our aspirations. We wrote about the life we dreamed together – a home filled with laughter, shared adventures, and a love that continued to evolve with each passing day. The words we penned under the moonlit sky were a testament to the depth of our connection, a promise etched in ink.

As the night deepened, we lay on the blanket, fingers intertwined, and watched the stars above. I whispered, "Rasika, each star in the sky holds a wish. What would you wish for, right here, right now?"

Rasika gazed at the vast expanse of the night sky, her voice soft, "I would wish for a lifetime of these moments with you Mayank – under the stars, on the sands of Anjuna."

My heart swelled with emotion, and I whispered my own wish, "I wish for a love that grows, an adventure that never ends, and a future where every sunset is as beautiful as this one."

Anjuna Beach, once a mere stretch of sand, became a sanctuary where our love found its voice under the blanket of stars. We wrapped ourselves in each other's warmth with the sound of the waves and the soft rustle of palm leaves. The night etched with the magic of Anjuna, the enchantment of love, and the promise of countless sunsets to come.

The Betrayal

It was the last day of our trip to goa, and I stood on Anjuna Beach, the moonlight casting long shadows across the sand. The air, once filled with the promise of romance, now carried an unsettling tension. With the ever-crashing sound of waves, I couldn't shake the feeling that something had shifted, that the narrative of our love story had taken an unexpected turn.

Earlier today when we woke up, Rasika told me that as the trip is about to end, she needs evidence that she came to Goa with her friends.

"Mayank our trip is about to end, what am I going to tell my parents?"

She told me looking into my eyes.

"What are you going to tell means? I did not get you."

I asked in curousity.

"Babe, I have told them about coming to Goa but with friends and not with you."

She informed and this time she was not making eye contact with me.

"So, what is the solution according to you?"

I further asked her.

"I forgot to tell you earlier but a few of my friends have also come to Goa and I am planning to go and meet them and will also take some photographs with them. I will show those photos to my parents."

She was speaking about friends I did not know about.

"Friends? Kaun aya hai Rasika?"

I was blank.

"U don't know them Mayank. They are my college buddies."

She replied.

"Okay"

I could not say anything, but I was not able to digest this narration.

"I will be back by the evening Mayank."

She was going for whole day, and this made me more suspicious as it had never happened before. It was 10 in the morning and as soon as she left in a rented scooty, I do not know why but I followed her. I did this carefully so that she may not know that I am following her. She told me about going to South Goa which was true as she did reach there. It took almost 40 minutes to reach South Goa from Anjuna Beach and she stopped outside a resort. I was keeping fair distance from her so that she may not doubt about my presence even by mistake. I saw that she took out her mobile and made a call. She was talking to someone, and the call ended after a couple of minutes. It did not take long and within a few minutes a guy came in a Bullet, and she smiled while looking at him. I assumed he might be one of the friends and may have come to take her to place they all were staying. But to my surprise she parked her scooty in that hotel and sat behind him and they drove off. My heart started beating so fast and I could not believe what my eyes were witnessing.

The guy was tall, Dark and was in shorts and Tshirt and she sat as close to him as she does with me. Seeing this made me cry and I literally started crying seeing Rasika with him. I was following them the whole time and they went to Palolem beach, the same place where we had gone at the first day of our arrival. I parked my scooty far from theirs and slowly walked behind them. He was holding her hand and she did not resist either, well is it really normal for a girl to roam around hand in hand with someone who is not her boyfriend?

"Dost hai dost hai."

I tried to calm my nerves even though somewhere deep inside I knew it was not right.

They further went inside the beach and this time he brought her closer holding her through waist and then it happened, he kissed her, and she kissed back. I am a kind of guy who finds kisses more passionate than actually having sex and they were involved in that activity only.

They spent half an hour at the beach and then left together. I did not dare to follow them further. Tired, lost and heartbroken I sat on a secluded part of the beach and cried my heart out.

Sun was about to set, and she had not called or messaged me yet, so I left the beach and drove towards my hotel. Doubt lingered, heavy and unwelcome, as I waited for Rasika under the moonlit sky.

When Rasika finally appeared, her smile felt like a façade, a mere flicker of what used to be. My attempt at small talk yielded forced responses, and the distance between us seemed to grow with every passing moment.

As we settled on the same blanket that had witnessed the beauty of our shared dreams, an invisible wall separated us. Rasika's gaze avoided mine, her eyes betraying a conflict that I struggled to comprehend.

"Is everything okay, Rasika?" I asked, a note of concern in my voice. Even though she had committed something which was so wrong to me, but I noticed that she had started feeling guilty.

Rasika hesitated, her fingers drawing patterns in the sand. "Mayank, there's something I need to tell you."

The weight of her words hung in the air, and my heart started beating faster. I urged her to continue, though the knot in my stomach tightened with each passing second.

"I... I've been seeing someone else," Rasika confessed, her voice barely above a whisper.

I felt as if the ground beneath me had shifted. The waves, once a comforting melody, now seemed to echo the pain in my heart. I struggled to process the words, the reality of her confession piercing through the beautiful scene around us.

My voice trembled as I asked, "I know. How long has this been going on?"

Rasika's eyes welled with remorse, "how do you know? Well, it started a few months ago. I never meant for it to happen, Mayank. It just... happened."

"I just know Rasika".

My mind raced with web of emotions – disbelief, anger, and a profound sadness that threatened to consume me.

"Why didn't you tell me sooner?" I questioned, my voice a mixture of hurt and frustration.

"I was scared," Rasika admitted, her gaze finally meeting mine. "I didn't want to hurt you. I thought I could sort things out on my own, but it's not fair to you. You deserve the truth."

The truth, though painful, hung between us like an unspoken verdict. With a heavy heart, I rose from the blanket and began to walk along the shoreline. Rasika followed, the distance between us expanding with each step.

The waves crashed against the shore, a symphony of endings and beginnings. I struggled to make sense of the shattered fragments of a love story that had once felt invincible with the weight of betrayal on my shoulders.

"Why, Rasika?" I finally asked, my voice tinged with a mix of anguish and resignation.

Rasika sighed, her shoulders sagging with the weight of guilt. "I don't have a simple answer, Mayank. I got lost, confused. It doesn't excuse what I've done, but I need you to understand that it was never about you. It was about me trying to find something I thought was missing."

I turned to face her with a heaviness in my chest. The moonlight illuminated the tear-streaked path on Rasika's face, mirroring the internal turmoil that raged within me.

"You've shattered something that meant everything to me," I whispered, my voice breaking. "I never imagined our story would unravel like this. I thought I will write beautiful experiences of our goan vacation in my novel."

As the truth hung in the air, we stood on the beach, two figures enveloped by the vastness of the night. Anjuna, once witness to our dreams, became a silent spectator to the unraveling of a love that had once seemed boundless.

With a heavy heart, I turned away, realizing that the beach, the stars, and the moonlit sky could no longer contain the echoes of a love story that had lost its way. Rasika, standing alone on the shore, watched as I disappeared into the night.

Anjuna Beach, once a haven for love, now bore witness to the remnants of a connection that was crushed under the weight of unspoken betrayals. That was also the last day of our stay in Goa and with the heavy heart I packed my bag and took the flight back to Jabalpur.

Now guided by the wisdom of experience, I embraced the uncertainty of tomorrow with a newfound courage. Goa, once a reminder of shared moments, transformed into a canvas where I painted the strokes of my own narrative about the light and lock that was lost. The waves of Anjuna Beach, though still whispering tales of love and loss, became echoes of a chapter closed—a reminder that, sometimes, the most profound stories are the ones we write for ourselves.

Making Out in Train?

It all started when we were travelling to Mumbai. I have told you everything about the Goa trip and the shocking revealation of Rasika's affair which broke my heart badly, but something else happened while travelling too. We took the plane to Goa from Mumbai, but before that we had a train from Jabalpur to Mumbai. I sat in the same train from Satna, and it was running towards Mumbai via Jabalpur.

It was our habit of booking corner seats in movie theatres and in trains our favourite seats were side lower and side upper of Second AC couches. The reason we liked these seats was the privacy it offers. In a second AC seat of a train there are curtains and if you have got the side lower and side upper seats of the same compartment, then it literally becomes a small personal cabin of yours. Even though there are no doors in this arrangement, but the curtains are there to offer complete privacy. So, we were travelling from Jabalpur to Mumbai and once we were done with the luggage and all, Rasika took the side lower seat, and I went above on the same side upper seat. Jabalpur to Mumbai is a 15-hour jounrney and we started in the evening. She had brought the dinner packed from our favourite 70 MM restaurant and we had it on her seat only. Since all co passengers were still awake so I went up to my seat again and she stayed in the lower seat.

It was 11 PM and all the lights were off in our couch. I was trying to sleep but it was not easy to sleep in a moving train, at least not for me. Having trouble sleeping, I looked down at Rasika's seat peeking through the corner of the curtain. She was also awake, and she noticed me immediately.

"You are also awake?"

She asked looking and smiling at me.

"It's moving badly yar, the train."

I replied smiling back at her.

"Come here na. Let's make the best use of this movement" She invited me to her seat with a wink.

"Are you mad? Someone might see us." I was afraid to join her.

"Everyone is sleeping can't you hear them snore?"

She was confident and persistant.

Hesitant, excited and nervous, I somehow gathered all my courage and went to her seat. Side lower and upper are having same length as that of the other seats but these seats are not as wide as others. It is just not possible for two full growns to lay side by side in that seat.

"Ban nahi raha hai let me come on top."

Saying this she came over me. I was now getting aroused and was nervous too since there was only this thin curtain between us and anyone passing nearby. Even though I was afraid but inside a moving train being with her in that side lower seat was making me so excited. We were looking into each other's eyes, and it did not take us long to start kissing.

"I want you now Mayank."

She whispered while still kissing me.

"I want you too Rasika but its too risky here."

I tried to bring her to the sense.

"I do not care. Risk lo ya Riksha Chalao."

She was determined and started giggling.

"Shhhh... You are mad, keep quite or somneone may hear us."

I tried to keep the noise levels down.

She didn't care what I said to her and within a few minutes we were both topless and seeing her sitting above me in the moving train that too topless was one of the most exciting things which I had ever witnessed in my whole life.

"You are so hot. I cannot believe what we are doing."

I was amazed with the scene in front of me. The girl every guy in our batch wanted to be with was sitting topless over me inside a moving train.

"Let's do it Mayank."

Saying this she got rid off the remaining piece of clothing of hers and it happened as she started making the moves. I was in the seventh heaven as this was something I had never even imagined in my dreams, making out in a moving train that too just behind a thin curtain. Forbidden acts often excite you more and I was realizing it today. The excitement was at peak and it was not long before I started saying,

"Rasika Stop now or get off, I cannot control anymore."

I tried to stop as the tremendous excitement was making it almost impossible for me to hold further.

"Rasika I am serious get off I cannot control anymore."

She did not listen to me and the next moment I was done.

She smiled looking at my relieved face.

"You are a mad mad girl."

I said smiling and kissing her. Soon we heard footspets approaching and we quickly got dressed. We sat in silence and waited for them to pass. It was the railways police force armed guard who was just passing by to check everything was normal. As soon as he passed, I went up to my seat.

Even today when I look back at this incident, I feel goosebumps. It is one of the few memories I cannot forget ever with each detail still as fresh as it happened yesterday.

Seed is Sown?

The atmosphere in the hotel I was staying in Jabalpur hung heavy with the unspoken weight of revelation. Rasika, her eyes holding a mixture of anxiety and anticipation, sat across me. The pregnancy test lay on the table between us, its result was a life-altering.

"Positive," she murmured, her voice tinged with uncertainty, anticipation, and perhaps a hint of apprehension. The weight of her words hangs heavy in the air, suffocating the already strained atmosphere between us.

My hands trembled as I reached for the test, turning it to face us. The positive sign felt like a seismic shift, a sudden departure from the plans we had laid out for our lives.

Rasika broke the silence, her voice a whisper, "Mayank, what do we do now?"

I took a deep breath. "We need to talk about our options, Rasika. This changes everything."

As she approached me with the pregnancy test in hand, my mind raced with a whirlwind of thoughts and emotions.

Shock, disbelief, anger, and perhaps even a glimmer of hope intermingled within me, creating a web of conflicting feelings. Discovering infidelity can be a profoundly distressing experience, compounded by the complexity of emotions that follow such a betrayal.

I stared at the pregnancy test in her trembling hands, the lines confirming a future forever altered. But amidst the chaos, a part of me wondered: is this the culmination of my love, a symbol of a bond that transcended betrayal? Or is it merely another layer of deceit to manipulate my emotions and salvage a fractured relationship?

"What do you want me to do?" she asked, her eyes pleading for answer.

I struggled to find my voice amidst the turmoil, grappling with the situation. Even our future was uncertain and here we were to take decision about bringing someone to this life or not.

In the midst of the chaos, I thought to take a logical approach and decision which required time.

"I need time," I finally managed to utter.

Time to untangle the web of lies and deceit, time to heal the wounds inflicted upon my heart, and time to chart a new course of actions after her betrayal.

The conversation that unfolded was raw and unfiltered. We discussed the implications of parenthood at this juncture of our lives – the impact on our careers, the financial strain, and the emotional readiness required for such a profound responsibility. The reality of our situation loomed, forcing us to confront the complexities of a decision that would reshape our future.

After hours of discussion, it became clear that, at this time, bringing a child into the world was not feasible. Though entwined by love, we faced the stark reality that our dreams, careers, and aspirations were the priorities.

Amidst the challenging conversation, my phone buzzed with an appointment reminder. Rasika glanced at me. "The clinic appointment," I said, confirming that we had arrived at a decision.

The clinic, with our hushed conversations, became the setting for a difficult choice. We sat in the waiting room, our hands intertwined, finding solace in each other's silent support. Our names were called, marking the beginning of a journey neither of us had imagined. I was in great dilemma as the current situation was a bit too much for me. She had recently confessed about the affair with her old college mate and here she was pregnant. I just did not know what to do but I was sure that I still loved her.

The doctor, empathetic yet professional, guided us through the process, explaining the options available and the potential emotional and physical implications. It was a whirlwind of information that left me and Rasika grappling with the complexity of our decision.

In the procedure room, I sat beside Rasika acting like a silent pillar of strength in that situation. The air was heavy with a mix of tension and shared grief. The medical professionals navigated the delicate process with care.

As the procedure concluded, a profound silence enveloped us. Our eyes met, mirroring the complexity of emotions we couldn't articulate. Leaving the clinic, the weight of our shared experience lingered in the air.

In the days that followed, we faced a mix of emotions – grief, relief, guilt, and a quiet acknowledgment of the choice we had made. The path to healing was a rocky one, and we leaned on each other for support, navigating the aftermath of our decision.

Conversations about the future became more deliberate, our dreams and aspirations not forgotten but momentarily overshadowed by the reality of the present. We sought solace in the fact that, as a team, we had faced an unexpected challenge and made a decision that was both practical and necessary.

As time passed, we found solace in our shared journey toward healing. We supported each other through moments of grief, understanding that our decision, though difficult, had been a product of love and mutual respect.

The experience, painful as it was, became a turning point in our relationship. We emerged from the shadows with a sense of empathy, a deepened bond that spoke of endurance, and a commitment to face whatever challenges lay ahead hand in hand.

Chapter IX

The Ebb of Love

The echoes of the abortion were not limited to the day of operation, but it shadowed over our once-vibrant love that had defined my relationship with Rasika for long. The aftermath had left an indelible mark, creating a gap that seemed to widen with each passing day.

Though we were physically present in each other's lives but found ourselves navigating through uncharted emotional territories. The pain, both physical and emotional, had taken its toll, leaving behind a landscape altered by the complexities of our horrific experience. Even though I was there supporting her throughout the period but what she had done in Goa was just not escaping my mind.

In the days that followed, conversations became dull, punctuated by long pauses and unspoken words. The intimacy that once flowed effortlessly had become rare between us. With my eyes carrying the weight of unspoken questions, I sought solace in understanding Rasika's emotional landscape.

Rasika, though grateful for my support, found herself grappling with the aftermath of our decision. Grief, guilt, and a sense of loss created an emotional undertow that threatened to pull her under. The tenderness that had once defined our connection seemed to be replaced by an unspoken distance that neither could bridge.

One evening, as we sat in our favourite restaurant, the weight of unspoken emotions hung in the air. Breaking the silence, I made an attempt to know what she was going through "Rasika, I can sense that something has changed between us. We need to talk about this."

Rasika, her gaze fixed on the flickering candlelight, nodded. "I know, Mayank. It's just… it's hard to put into words."

Vulnerable and seeking understanding, I expressed the pain of witnessing the love we had built unravel. Rasika, grappling with a sense of inadequacy and grief, acknowledged the emotional distance which was evident between us.

"It's not that I blame you, Rasika," I confessed, my voice a mix of frustration and yearning. "But I feel like we're strangers trying to navigate a shared history that has become too heavy to bear."

Rasika, tears glistening in her eyes, "I never wanted this distance between us, Mayank. It's like a part of me has shut down, and I don't know how to reconnect."

The restaurant, once a haven for our whispered confessions and shared dreams, became a witness to the unraveling of a connection that had once felt unbreakable.

In the days that followed, we attempted to navigate the fragile terrain of rebuilding. Yet, despite our regular efforts, the love that had once been our anchor seemed to be fading away. The intimacy, once second nature, now required effort, and the spontaneity that had defined our love story seemed like a distant memory.

"Rasika, I love you, but I can't ignore the fact that something has fundamentally changed. Can we find our way back?"

Rasika, her eyes reflecting a mix of regret and uncertainty, took a deep breath. "I don't know, Mayank. I want to, but I feel like a part of me is lost, and I'm not sure how to reclaim it."

The admission hung heavy, a realization that the love we had once taken for granted was missing.

As time passed, we faced the harsh reality that love, though resilient, could be forever altered by the trials of life. The shared history, once a source of strength, became a complex tapestry woven with threads of joy, pain, and unspoken compromises. The journey toward healing, though undertaken with sincerity, couldn't erase the scars that marked the landscape of our love.

In the quiet moments, as we navigated the uncharted waters of our relationship, we grappled with the realization that sometimes love, even when held in the highest regard, could transform into a bittersweet memory.

The dynamics of our relationship had shifted, a subtle undercurrent of tension that betrayed the weight of unspoken words. The intimacy that once defined our relationship now hung in the balance, threatened by the revelation that had shaken the foundations of our love. With a mix of hurt and confusion, I confronted Rasika about the affair that had come to light.

It started with a heated exchange; the air thick with unresolved emotions. Unable to contain the turmoil within, I asked the question that had been troubling me since the truth had surfaced. "Rasika, how could you do this? How could you betray us?"

Rasika, her eyes betraying a mix of guilt and defensiveness, hesitated before responding. "Mayank, I… I don't have an excuse. It was a mistake, a moment of weakness. I never meant to hurt you."

The admission hung in the air, leaving me grappling with the magnitude of her betrayal. The details spilled out – romantic meetings, whispered conversations, and a web of deceit that had unfolded and it was all about her being with someone else.

My anger erupted. "A mistake? Rasika, this is not a minor lapse in judgment. This is a breach of trust, a violation of everything we built together. How am I supposed to believe anything you say now?"

Rasika, her eyes welling with tears, attempted to bridge the growing chasm. "Mayank, please understand. I never stopped loving you. It was a moment of weakness, a fleeting distraction. I never wanted to ruin what we have."

I questioned the foundation upon which our relationship had been built. Rasika sought forgiveness in the midst of a storm that threatened to consume us both.

As the hours passed, the argument evolved into a painful dialogue about how that one incident has weaken our connection. With a mix of desperation and frustration in my voice, I demanded transparency. “How long has this been going on, Rasika? How many lies have we lived?”

Rasika, her shoulders sagging with the weight of guilt, admitted to a timeline that stretched beyond what I was expecting. She was continuously in touch with the guy from last two years but what happened in Goa was the first time. The unraveling truth became a tapestry of betrayal, leaving me to grapple with the harsh reality that the woman I loved had sought solace in the arms of another.

The emotional toll of the revelation left us both exhausted, yet the conversation persisted into the night. Further seeking answers, I asked the question, “Why? Why did you do this?”

Rasika, tears streaming down her face, attempted to articulate the complex web of emotions that had led to her betrayal. “Mayank, I felt neglected, unimportant. It wasn’t about you; it was about me trying to fill a void that I thought existed in our relationship. I was wrong, and I regret it every day.”

The trust we had once shared now lay shattered, and the woman I thought I knew seemed like a stranger.

As the weeks passed, we faced a crossroads. The decision to either repair our fractured love or acknowledge the irreparable damage which our relationship was suffering with. Torn between the love I once felt and the betrayal I couldn’t forget, I confronted Rasika with a question that hung like a pendulum between our destinies.

“Can we move past this, Rasika? Can our love survive this storm?”

Rasika, her eyes reflecting a mix of remorse and determination, nodded. “Mayank, I love you. I made a terrible mistake, and I can’t change the past. But I’m willing to do whatever it takes to rebuild our trust, to rebuild us.”

The road ahead was uncertain, fraught with the challenges of healing wounds that ran deep. I and Rasika, though scarred by the tempest that had shaken our love, faced the choice to either let go of what remained or embark on the a difficult journey of rebuilding. The echoes of our shared pain resonated, a haunting reminder that the love we once knew had been forever altered by the choices we made.

The Breakup Call?

It was April 2016 and I was still posted in Satna branch of Unite Bank of India and my relationship and decision of staying or not with Rasika was still hung in the air. As usual the night unfolded in darkness, mirroring the turmoil within my heart. In the depth of my heartache, I reached for my phone, to connect to Rasika – the woman with whom my relationship lingered in the delicate balance between uncertainty and unspoken connection. Unlike before, we did not talk every day, infact I cannot even remember the last time we talked on phone.

As the phone rang, each passing second felt like an eternity, the anticipation building with each heartbeat. Rasika, on the other end, answered,

“Mayank?” Her tone with familiarity and an unspoken tension.

"Yeah, it's me," I responded, my words carrying the weight of emotions I had long kept submerged beneath the surface. The night, once a canvas for celebration, now became the backdrop to a conversation that would lay bare the complexities of our relationship.

In the stillness of the night, I and Rasika embarked on a dialogue with all aspects of our relationship and the future course of action. The unspoken tension that had lingered between us now found a voice,

"Rasika, I don't know where we stand,"

"It's like we're stuck in this limbo, neither moving forward nor fully letting go."

I confessed, what I was actually feeling.

Rasika, on the other end of the line, sighed – a sigh pregnant with the weight of acknowledgment. "Mayank, you know it's not that simple. We have our own lives, our own paths, yet there's this thread that binds us together."

The thread –the connection we couldn't sever, even when the road ahead seemed unclear. With heavy heart I said, "Rasika, we can't keep dancing around this ambiguity. It's tearing me apart. I need to know if there's a future for us or if it's time to finally let go."

The silence that followed was killing me as I knew where the discussion was going. Rasika, choosing her words with a precision finally spoke. "Mayank, you know I care about you. But the distance, the different cities, our respective lives and recent developments – they complicate things. I can't promise a future, and I can't deny the connection we share."

Grappling with the honesty that hung in the air, I felt a lump forming in my throat. The weight of unspoken expectations collided with the reality of our circumstances. "So, what do we do? Keep drifting in this undefined space?"

Rasika, her voice softening, replied, "I wish it were simpler, but life rarely is. Maybe we need to give ourselves the space to figure things out. It doesn't mean we have to let go completely, but we can't keep holding onto something that might never fully materialize."

The words, though pragmatic, cut through my heart. The ache was unbearable yet, amidst the pain, there was a strange sense of relief – the relief of finally confronting the ambiguity that had haunted our relationship.

As the conversation unfolded, we delved into the details of our individual lives. Rasika shared the challenges of her career, the demands of a life in a different city, and the unforeseen twists that had shaped her journey. In turn my narrative was about my banking career, the highs and lows, and the loneliness that sometimes accompanied my professional pursuits.

Amidst the deep conversation, a strange sense of closure began to emerge. The acknowledgment that our relationship might not fit into a neat, predetermined box became the foundation for a new understanding. The unspoken tension that had lingered between us transformed into a shared acceptance of the uncertainties that lay ahead.

As the night progressed, we navigated the terrain of shared memories. We revisited the laughter that had echoed through the phone lines during late-night conversations, the whispered confessions and the moments of shared camaraderie that defined our relationship.

It was an acknowledgment of the love that had flourished in the silences between words, the shared dreams that had woven a bond, and the recognition that sometimes love, in all its complexity, couldn't be neatly confined to the boundaries of definitions.

With the dawn approaching on the horizon, we reached a juncture in our conversation. The night, which had been a canvas for the exploration of emotions, now held the promise of a new beginning. The acknowledgment that our relationship needed space to breathe, to evolve, became the catalyst for a mutual decision.

"Mayank," Rasika began, her voice a gentle reassurance, "maybe it's time for both of us to step back, to give ourselves the space to grow individually. It doesn't mean we have to cut ties completely, but perhaps we need to release ourselves from the expectations that have bound us."

Though grappling with the ache of letting go, I felt a strange sense of clarity in Rasika's words. The acknowledgement that our relationship needed to evolve, to adapt to the changing landscapes of our lives, became a bridge to a new phase of understanding.

As the call concluded, I was left with a mixture of emotions. The ache of a love that couldn't be neatly defined, the relief of confronting the ambiguity, and the acceptance that sometimes love, in all its complexities, required the courage to let go.

The night call which started in uncertainty was concluded with transformative conversation. Though heartbroken, I found a strange sense of peace in the acknowledgment that our relationship, like the ebb and flow of life, was a dynamic force that needed the freedom to evolve.

As I laid in the darkness, the weight of the conversation settling over me, I felt a strange mix of emotions. The ache of unfulfilled expectations lingered, but so did the promise of a new beginning – a beginning that unfolded in the uncertain terrain of self-discovery and the resilience to embrace the ever-changing tides of life.

Chapter X

The Farewell

Months had passed since I and Rasika embarked on the journey of self-discovery, each navigating through the life independently. The echoes of our late-night conversations, shared dreams, and unspoken connection lingered in the recesses of our memories. As the seasons changed, so did the dynamics of our relationship, evolving into a phase that now begged for closure.

The decision to meet, to finally bid farewell, was both an inevitability and a choice born out of the recognition that the threads that once bound us needed to be gently unraveled.

It was first of August 2017 and the meeting was set in our favourite 70 MM restaurant for the one last time. A Café that held the echoes of our shared laughter and witnessed some of the best moments that we spent together in Jabalpur.

As Rasika entered the café, her presence carried a blend of familiarity and the weight of unspoken complexities. Our eyes met, and for a moment, time seemed to stand still as I remembered the moment when I first saw her in SBTC. The connection we had shared, once vibrant and filled with promises, now hung in the air like a fragile thread.

"Mayank," Rasika greeted. "It's been a while."

"Yeah," I responded, a subtle acknowledgment that carried the weight of the months we had spent apart. The café, once a setting for casual meetings and shared moments, now became the backdrop for a conversation that would redefine the boundaries of our relationship.

As we settled into our favourite seats at the quiet corner of the café, the atmosphere held a tension that mirrored the unspoken complexities of our emotions. The menu, which we almost had remembered after trying most of the dishes, became a momentary distraction as we navigated the nuances of small talk – an attempt to bridge the gap between familiarity and the uncharted territory that lay ahead.

The conversation, initially started with how we were doing, gradually delved into the heart of the matter. My eyes reflecting a blend of resignation and sincerity, broached the unspoken topic that lingered between us.

"Rasika, we can't keep dancing around this. Our lives have taken different paths, and it's time we acknowledge that," I began, the weight of my words hanging in the air.

Rasika, her gaze meeting mine with a mixture of understanding and regret, nodded. "Mayank, I know. It's not easy, but it's something we need to face."

The acknowledgment, though spoken with a calm resolve, couldn't conceal the undercurrent of emotions.

As the restaurant hummed with the ambient sounds of quiet conversations and the clinking of cutlery, we began to unpack the complexities of our individual journeys. The months apart had carved new chapters in our lives – new experiences, new challenges, and a subtle transformation that colored the canvas of our individual narratives.

"I've learned a lot about myself in these months," I admitted, my gaze fixed on a point in the distance. "There's a part of me that will always care about you, but I've also come to realize that our connection, as beautiful as it was, might not fit into the lives we're building separately."

Rasika, her eyes reflecting a similar sentiment, responded, "Mayank, I've had my share of realizations too. Our connection was special, but it's clear that our paths are diverging. We owe it to ourselves to embrace the changes and let go of what was."

The conversation was guided by a mutual desire for honesty and acceptance. We revisited the shared memories, the late-night confessions, and the dreams that once held the promise of a shared future. Each word became a steppingstone in the journey toward closure, a closure that was both liberating and heart-wrenching.

As we navigated the terrain of our emotions, we confronted the complexities that had long lingered beneath the surface. The distance, the changing dynamics of our lives, and the acknowledgment that love, in all its forms, sometimes required the courage to let go – all became integral facets of our conversation.

"Mayank," Rasika began, her voice tinged with a mixture of regret and acceptance, "I want you to know that what we had was special. It wasn't just a fleeting connection; it was a chapter in our lives that shaped us."

With my eyes gaze meeting Rasika's with a blend of gratitude and sorrow, I responded, "I feel the same way, Rasika. You were a significant part of my journey, and I'll always carry the memories we created together."

I and Rasika, in bidding farewell to our shared history, confronted the harsh reality that sometimes love, even when genuine and profound, couldn't transcend the changes that life brought.

The café, now a witness to the culmination of our conversation, held a strange sense of finality. The unspoken tension that had lingered between us replaced by a shared understanding that the time had come to release the threads that once bound us.

As we rose from our seats, we exchanged a glance that held a silent acknowledgment. The café, once a setting for shared moments, now became the stage for a farewell that echoed with the gravity of unspoken goodbyes.

As we stepped outside into the cool evening breeze of Jabalpur, the weight of the decision settled over us. Embarking on the next chapters of our lives, we carried the echoes of a connection with ourselves that had shaped our journeys in ways both profound and transformative.

The farewell, though difficult, became a gateway to new beginnings. With a shared understanding and a profound respect for the love that once flourished between us, we embraced the uncertainty of the future. The café, now fading into the backdrop of our shared history, became a stepping stone toward the evolution of our individual narratives – a narrative that, though separate, would forever carry the imprint of a connection that had once blossomed in the quiet corners of our hearts.

The air hung heavy with unspoken emotions as we stepped out of the café, the door closing behind us with a quiet finality. The farewell, though necessary, had left us both suspended in a space where the echoes of shared history collided with the stark reality of parting ways.

Silence settled between us, a heavy blanket that enveloped the air with the weight of unspoken words. The city, bustling around us, seemed oblivious to the quiet storm that raged within me and Rasika. The farewell, though mutual shared sentiment that spoke volumes without the need for words.

With my hands tucked into the pockets, I cast a glance at Rasika. Her eyes, once a repository of shared confessions and laughter, now was having expressions which I was completely unaware of.

“I didn’t think it would be this hard,” I confessed, my voice carrying the vulnerability of a heart in transition. “We both knew this was coming, but somehow, the reality of saying goodbye feels heavier than I imagined.”

Rasika, her gaze fixed on a distant point, nodded. “It’s like we’re closing a chapter, and even though we know it’s the right thing to do, it doesn’t make it any less painful.”

The city, usually a backdrop to shared adventures, now became a silent witness to the quiet sorrow that marked our steps. As we began to walk along the dimly lit streets of Sadar, we found ourselves grappling with the uncharted terrain of emotions.

"It's strange, isn't it?" Rasika said, her voice carrying a hint of nostalgia. "We spent so much time building something beautiful, and now we're unraveling it in a matter of moments."

I nodded; my gaze fixed on the ground beneath my feet. "Life has a way of leading us through these cycles – moments of connection, of shared dreams, and then the painful process of letting go. It's the letting go that's the hardest part."

The city, though bathed in the glow of streetlights, seemed to dim around us. We continued to walk, the rhythmic sound of our footsteps echoing in the silence.

"I'll miss you," I admitted, my voice a whisper in the stillness of the night. "Even though we're choosing different paths, a part of me will always carry the warmth of what we had."

Rasika, her eyes glistening with unshed tears, replied, "I'll miss you too, Mayank. You were more than just a part of my life; you were a significant chapter that shaped who I am. I do not know if you will ever believe me or not, but I have never loved anyone as much as I loved you but unfortunately that love is missing now."

The confession, though heartfelt, couldn't alleviate the sorrow that lingered between us. The farewell, though steeped in mutual understanding, exposed the vulnerability of our hearts. The shared history, now a tapestry of memories, became both a solace and a source of heartache as we navigated the winding streets.

As we reached a park, illuminated by the soft glow of lampposts, we found an empty bench. We sat in silence, the distance between us a testament to the emotional space we needed to navigate. The park, once a place for laughter and stolen moments, became a space where the farewell unfolded beneath the swaying branches.

With my eyes fixed on the distant cityscape, I felt the weight of the sadness settle within me.

"I want you to be happy," I said, breaking the silence. "Even though it hurts, I want you to find the joy and fulfillment you deserve."

Rasika, a tear escaping the corner of her eye, responded, "And I want the same for you, Mayank. We both deserve a chance at happiness, even if it means walking separate paths."

The acknowledgment hung in the air, a harsh truth that resonated in the quiet corners of the park. The bench, once a seat for shared conversations, now bore witness to the shared understanding that sometimes love required the courage to release the ties that bound.

The night wore on, I and Rasika, our hearts heavy with the weight of farewells, sat in shared contemplation. The farewell, though marked by sadness, held the promise of new beginnings – the promise that in letting go, we were making space for the unwritten chapters that awaited us.

As we rose from the bench, we exchanged a lingering glance. The park, now a silent witness to our shared history, faded into the background. The farewell.

Echoes of Heartbreak

In the quiet corners of my heart a sorrow storm was killing me from inside as I grappled with the shattering reality of my breakup with Rasika. The echoes of our shared laughter and the warmth of our connection were replaced by a profound ache.

The breakup had left me bewildered and heartbroken. It was on a gloomy evening, the sky overcast with clouds mirroring the turmoil in my soul, that I found myself seated in a dimly lit cafe. The aroma of coffee, once a comforting scent, now mingled with the bitter tang of heartache.

I whispered to myself, "How did we get here? Everything felt so right, and now… it's all gone."

The memories of our time together played like a film in my mind—a reel of laughter, shared dreams, and the intimacy that had once made us feel inseparable. The cafe, once a place of shared smiles and stolen glances, now witnessed the silent mourning of a love that had slipped through my fingers.

My phone, an instrument that had once buzzed with messages of affection, now felt like a heavy weight in my pocket. The last message from Rasika, a heartbreaking farewell that left more questions than answers, taunted me like a haunting melody.

The breakup was not sudden but it left me grappling with a sense of loss that felt too raw to comprehend. I traced back the steps of our relationship, searching for clues, trying to pinpoint the fracture that led to breaking of our once-unbreakable bond.

"Was it something I said? Did I miss the signs? Where did it all go wrong?"

The unanswered questions swirled in my mind, a tempest of doubt and self-reflection. In the solitude of my thoughts, I replayed our last conversation.

"Was there a moment, a sentence, that changed everything? Or was it a gradual unraveling that I failed to see?"

The pain of the breakup, a sharp ache that seemed to radiate from my chest, transcended the confines of the cafe. It badly affected every facet of my life, casting a shadow over the memories I once held dear. The days that followed felt like an endless procession of numbness, the world moving around me while I was stuck with the breakup in my mind. Friends offered solace, their words of comfort echoing in the background, but the void left by Rasika could not be filled by anyone or anything.

My routine, once defined by shared moments and the anticipation of seeing Rasika's call, now felt like a mechanical procession. The laughter of colleagues, the chatter of passersby, all seemed to be part of a distant reality that I could no longer fully inhabit.

In the quiet solitude of my room, I confronted the memories of our shared life—the photographs, the gifts, the echoes of a love that once felt eternal. Each item, once a cherished token of our connection, now served as a painful reminder of what was lost.

"How do you move on when every corner of your life is filled with memories of someone you loved?" I whispered to myself.

The ache of heartbreak, an emotional undertow that threatened to pull me under, intensified as I grappled with the realization that the person, I had envisioned a future with was no longer a part of my present.

The nights were the hardest. In the silent hours, when the world outside was shrouded in darkness, I found myself wrestling with the ghosts of what once was. The bed we had shared, now a vast expanse of emptiness, became a battlefield where dreams and reality clashed in the theater of my mind.

"How do you silence the echoes of a love that lingers in every corner of your heart?"

I whispered in darkness.

The well-intentioned advice of friends and colleagues, though offered with genuine care, felt like distant murmurs in the symphony of my pain. The journey of healing, a path paved with the edges of shattered dreams, unfolded slowly. The wounds, though less raw, bore the scars of a love that had left an indelible mark.

As the seasons changed, so did I. My laughter, though tinged with the echoes of what once was, became a testament to the resilience of the human spirit.

"Life goes on, they say. I just never imagined it would be without her."

I said to myself looking at the mirror. The scars of heartbreak, though never fully erased, became a part of my story—a story that continued to unfold, not as a sequel to what was lost but as a narrative of resilience and the capacity to endure.

In the quiet moments of reflection, I acknowledged the bittersweet truth that love, in all its forms, shapes and reshapes the contours of our lives. The café, once a witness to the unraveling of a love story, now stood as a backdrop to a man who, though forever changed, found solace in the quiet melody of moving forward.

"Maybe one day, the ache will subside, and the memories will be tender reminders instead of open wounds. Until then, I'll navigate this journey, one step at a time."

And so, with a heart still healing, I promised myself to continue my journey marked by the ebb and flow of emotions, the echoes of a love that once defined me, and the quiet strength found in the aftermath of heartbreak.

Back to Beginning

Life is often a journey filled with unexpected twists and turns, leading us down paths we never imagined we would traverse. For me, this journey took me back to my roots, to the quaint town of Katni, where I had spent my formative years before venturing out into the world. After five years of navigating the bustling streets of Singrauli and Satna as a bank officer, fate had a different plan for me, bringing me back to where it all began.

It was in the year 2008 when I bid farewell to Katni, my home, to pursue higher education in the neighboring city of Jabalpur. Little did I know that those years would shape me in ways I could never have anticipated. As I returned to Katni in September 2017 after nine long years, a rush of nostalgia engulfed me, each corner of the town whispering tales of my childhood and adolescence.

One of the most heartwarming aspects of returning to my hometown was reconnecting with old friends, comrades from the battlefield of school days. The familiar faces, now grown and matured, greeted me with warmth and excitement, reminiscing about our shared memories and the dreams we once dared to dream. It was as though time had stood still in some ways, and yet, we had all evolved in our own unique ways, shaped by the experiences life had bestowed upon us.

My transfer from Satna to Madhavnagar Katni branch marked the beginning of a new chapter in my professional journey. As I stepped into the bustling corridors of the Madhavnagar branch, the air was charged with the energy of a fresh start. The unfamiliar faces and the hum of activity signaled the onset of a different rhythm – a rhythm that would define my experience in this new setting.

The first encounter with Mr. Mittal, my new branch manager at the Madhavnagar branch, unfolded with an unexpected blend of humor and warmth that set the tone for a unique camaraderie. As I entered the manager's cabin, I was greeted by a funny laugh that echoed through the room, instantly relieving traces of nervousness.

"Mayank, my man! Welcome to the Madhavnagar branch!" Mr. Mittal exclaimed, rising from his chair.

The ice was broken, not by the usual formalities, but by Mr. Mittal's infectious sense of humor. Initially unsure of what to expect, I found myself drawn into a dynamic conversation that seamlessly blended professionalism with a light-hearted spirit. As we discussed the routine and branch operations, Mr. Mittal managed to infuse each topic with a touch of humor.

"You'll find, Mayank, that a good laugh is the secret ingredient to a well-functioning branch," Mr. Mittal remarked, his eyes twinkling with a mischievous glint.

I couldn't help but appreciate the refreshing approach Mr. Mittal brought to his managerial role. The conventional barriers between a manager and an employee seemed to dissolve, replaced by a sense of camaraderie that bordered on the familiarity of an elder brother.

Beyond the professional realm, Mr. Mittal took a genuine interest in the well-being of his team. Lunch breaks became an extension of the camaraderie forged during meetings, with Mr. Mittal regaling the team with entertaining stories from his own experiences. His role as a mentor and elder brother became increasingly evident as I navigated through my new responsibilities. In moments of challenge or uncertainty, Mr. Mittal's office door was always open, not just for professional guidance but for a friendly chat that often began with a humorous remark to lighten the mood.

One of the highlights of my new experience was the cultural immersion that Madhavnagar offered specially with the majority of Sindhi community. The city, rich in history and traditions, unfolded its tapestry of festivals, fairs, and local events which Sindhis celebrated. Eager to embrace the spirit of my new surroundings, I found myself participating in the festivities that celebrated the cultural diversity of Madhavnagar.

As I settled into my role as a bank officer in Katni, I quickly realized the profound advantage of being a local. My intimate knowledge of the town and its people proved to be an invaluable asset in navigating the daily routines of the branch. Whether it was understanding the intricacies of local customs or anticipating the needs of the community, my roots ran deep, anchoring me to the fabric of Katni's society.

One of the most rewarding aspects of my work was the opportunity to extend a helping hand to friends, relatives, and colleagues alike. Whether it was facilitating a loan for an entrepreneur or offering financial advice to a family in need, I took immense pride in being able to make a meaningful difference in the lives of those around me. The sense of fulfillment that came from knowing that I was contributing to the well-being of my community was unparalleled, reinforcing my belief in the power of service and compassion.

As the seasons changed and the years rolled by, Katni became more than just a place of residence; it became my sanctuary, a sanctuary where I found solace amidst the chaos of the world. The bonds I forged and the memories I created served as a constant reminder of the enduring power of home, a beacon of light guiding me through the darkest of nights.

In retrospect, my return to Katni was not just a physical homecoming; it was a journey of self-discovery, a testament to the enduring bonds of friendship and community. It taught me the importance of embracing one's roots, of finding strength in familiarity, and of never forgetting the values instilled in us by the places we call home.

As I look back on those years spent in Katni, I am filled with gratitude for the experiences lived and the lessons learned. It is said that home is where the heart is, and for me, Katni will forever be the beating heart that continues to nourish my soul, no matter where life's journey may lead.

Unforeseen Attention

Navigating the delicate terrain of interpersonal relationships can be a difficult task, especially in the aftermath of a breakup. As I found myself in the familiar surroundings of Katni, nursing the wounds of a fractured romance, I was hesitant to engage in any new romantic journey. However, fate had a peculiar way of testing my resolve, as I soon found myself entangled in unexpected encounters with the lady customers of the madhavnagar branch where I worked.

Despite my best efforts to maintain a professional demeanor, I found myself on the receiving end of flirtatious advances from some of the lady customers, particularly those of Sindhi descent. Their beauty was undeniable, and it was difficult to resist their charms. Each encounter was like a dance of temptation, a delicate balance between propriety and desire.

Their subtle gestures and playful banter served as a constant reminder of the allure of romance, stirring dormant emotions that I had hoped to keep at bay. It was a test of willpower, a battle between the heart and the mind, as I grappled with the temptation to have a taste of forbidden fruit.

Despite the inherent risks involved, there was an undeniable thrill in the air, a sense of excitement that coursed through my veins with each encounter. It was as though fate had conspired to challenge my resolve, presenting me with opportunities to explore the boundaries of my own desires.

As time passed and wounds began to heal, I gradually found the courage to confront my fears and insecurities head-on. While the allure of romance still lingered in the air, I came to realize that true fulfillment could only be found within oneself, independent of external validation or fleeting pleasures. It was a journey of self-discovery, a process of reclaiming my sense of agency and autonomy in the face of adversity.

In retrospect, my encounters with the flirtatious lady customers served as a reminder of the complexity of human emotions and the unpredictable nature of desire. While the temptation to indulge in fleeting moments of passion may have been alluring, it was ultimately the strength of character and resilience that guided me through the storm. And though the scars of heartbreak may have left their mark, they served as a testament to the resilience of the human spirit, a reminder that even in the darkest of times, there is always hope for a brighter tomorrow.

The atmosphere in the Madhavnagar branch began to change. Customers, previously accustomed to a more transactional relationship with the bank, now specifically asked for me by name.

It wasn't just the younger clientele; even some more seasoned customers couldn't resist engaging in the light chitchat with me. The bank, once a space primarily associated with financial transactions, transformed into a theater where playful exchanges and charming repartees unfolded amidst the counters and service desks.

Despite the flirtatious undertones, my interactions with lady customers were always respectful. I maintained a balance between acknowledging the lighthearted banter and ensuring that the professional atmosphere of the bank was preserved. Colleagues often marveled at my ability to engage in playful banter without ever crossing the line into inappropriate territory.

As the playful exchanges became a part of the daily routine, my desk evolved into a space where more than just financial transactions unfolded. It became a hub of social interaction, where customers felt comfortable engaging in light banter and sharing smiles amidst discussions about their financial needs. The atmosphere, though unconventional for a banking setting, contributed to a positive and welcoming ambiance within the branch.

Mr. Mittal, the branch manager, observed the evolving dynamics with approving gaze. He recognized that the unique atmosphere, shaped by my unintentional charm, contributed to a more relaxed and customer-friendly environment. The lady customers, in particular, seemed to appreciate the departure from the stereotypical seriousness associated with banking.

One of the more intriguing aspects of my interactions with lady customers was the genuine camaraderie that developed over time. It wasn't just about flirtation; it was about creating connections and fostering a sense of ease within the banking space.

In the grand scheme of things, the flirtatious encounters added an unexpected layer of charm to the Madhavnagar branch. The lady customers, in their playful exchanges with me, found not just a banker but a friendly face who made their banking experiences memorable. My unintentional role as the charismatic banker, though lighthearted, underscored the idea that a welcoming and personable approach could redefine the narrative of what banking could be – an experience that went beyond the transactional and embraced the nuances of human interaction

Chapter XI

Ishita

It was a crisp autumn evening in 2017, and the Madhavnagar branch was adorned with the festive spirit of Dussehra. The air was infused with the aroma of incense, and the distant sounds of drums and celebrations echoed through the town. Amidst this vibrant atmosphere, I found myself at my desk, immersed in the routine tasks of the day, unaware that the upcoming interaction would mark the beginning of a unique chapter.

As the door to the bank swung open, a burst of laughter and the rustle of traditional clothing announced the arrival of someone special. In walked Ishita, a young woman with an infectious smile that seemed to light up the room. Wearing a vibrant kurta, she exuded an aura of youthful energy that perfectly complemented the festive ambiance.

Ishita approached the service desk, her eyes scanning the surroundings as if taking in the atmosphere of the bank. Engrossed in paperwork, I looked up just in time to catch the first glimpse of her. The festive spirit that enveloped Madhavnagar seemed to find a reflection in Ishita's lively presence.

"Excuse me," Ishita said with a warm smile, capturing my attention. "I need to get an ATM card issued. Can you help me with that?"

Momentarily taken aback by the brightness of Ishita's smile, I quickly composed myself and replied, "Of course! I'd be happy to assist you. May I have your name and account details, please?"

As Ishita provided the necessary information, I couldn't help but notice the subtle excitement in her voice. It wasn't just about a routine banking task; there was an underlying enthusiasm that suggested a connection to the festive occasion and perhaps a hint of nostalgia.

Engaged in the transaction, I took the opportunity to strike up a conversation. "So, what brings you to the bank today, especially on such a festive day?" I inquired, a friendly curiosity coloring my words.

Ishita's eyes sparkled with a blend of mirth and sincerity. "Well, I'm actually studying in Bhopal, and I've come home for Dussehra. Thought it would be a good time to get some banking tasks sorted."

Dussehra, a festival of joy and victory, seemed to have brought not just celebrations but also a touch of serendipity to the Madhavnagar branch. As we continued with the formalities of the ATM card issuance, I found myself weaving the conversation beyond the confines of banking procedures.

"Must be nice to be back home for the festivities," I remarked, a genuine smile accompanying my words.

Ishita nodded, her eyes reflecting a mix of nostalgia and joy. "Absolutely! There's something special about celebrating Dussehra and Diwali in your hometown. The traditions, the colors, the festivities – it's a different feeling altogether."

The conversation flowed seamlessly, effortlessly transitioning between the practicalities of banking and the shared sentiment of celebrating festivals in one's hometown.

As the transaction neared completion, I handed over the freshly issued ATM card to Ishita, accompanied by a friendly wish for the ongoing festivities. "Here's your new card. Wishing you a joyful Dussehra and a wonderful stay in Madhavnagar!"

Ishita's gratitude was evident in her radiant smile. "Thank you, sir! I appreciate your help. And yes, looking forward to enjoying Dussehra to the fullest."

"Mayank." I introduced myself.

"Thank you Mayank." She replied and smiled.

Little did we know that this seemingly routine interaction would just be a starting point for connection that would extend beyond the confines of the bank. As Ishita left the branch, her footsteps echoed a melody of celebration, and I, still at my desk, couldn't shake off the feeling that something special had just unfolded.

In the days that followed, Ishita's visits to my branch became more frequent. Whether it was a routine transaction or a simple inquiry, she always seemed to gravitate toward my desk. She was in Katni for a long vacation and was only going to leave for Bhopal after Diwali. The connection, forged on the backdrop of Dussehra and our initial interaction, grew organically, evolving into a friendship that surpassed the boundaries of a typical customer-banker relationship.

The festive spirit that had initially brought us together continued to weave its magic into our interactions, creating a sense of camaraderie that felt more like a celebration than a routine banking task.

Our conversations, though often centered around banking matters, touched various topics. From shared experiences of celebrating festivals to discussions about life in Bhopal and Madhavnagar, we found ourselves effortlessly navigating between the personal and the practical.

The bank, once a space defined by the seriousness of financial transactions, now carried an undertone of celebration whenever Ishita stepped through its doors. Colleagues, noticing the camaraderie that had developed between me and Ishita, often exchanged knowing glances, acknowledging the unique dynamic.

Dussehra, the auspicious beginning that marked our first interaction, became a symbol of our growing friendship. The festival, with its spirit of triumph and joy, seemed to set the tone for the connection that continued to blossom between us.

Mr. Mittal, the branch manager, observed the blossoming friendship with an evil smile. One such day when Ishita was visiting our branch, I was surrounded by two other lady customers and coincidently all three of them including Ishita were young and beautiful. Mr. Mittal sent a message through an internal messanger that we use in bank,

"I do not know why but I feel one of them is going to be ur life partner."

I looked at him immediately after receiving and reading his message and he was smiling.

Soon after Ishita's regular visits we exchanged phone numbers and started chatting on WhatsApp, embarking on a journey that would redefine the way we communicated and forged a unique bond. Little did we know that this seemingly innocent exchange of numbers would become the catalyst for a series of phone calls that would unravel the layers of our personalities and foster a connection that went beyond the surface.

The first phone call is a tentative exploration, both me and Ishita navigated the uncharted waters of phone conversations. The initial awkwardness gave way to laughter as we discovered shared interests, common experiences, and the subtle nuances.

Mayank: (laughing) Ishita, you won't believe the number of times I've misplaced my keys. It's become a running joke in my life.

Ishita: (giggling) Well, Mayank, you're not alone. I once spent an entire morning looking for my phone while talking on it.

The laughter became a bridge that connected us, forging a comfort that transcended the physical distance between our conversations. As the phone calls became a regular part of our routine, we found ourselves delving into deeper discussions about life, aspirations, and the experiences that have shaped us.

Ishita: (thoughtfully) Mayank, what's something you've always wanted to do but haven't had the chance to?

Mayank: (reflecting) Travel, I guess. There's so much of the world to explore, and I've only scratched the surface.

Ishita: (excitedly) Well, consider that a plan in the making. We should plan a trip together someday.

The prospect of shared adventures became a topic of anticipation, our conversations weaving dreams and possibilities that extend beyond the confines of daily routines.

As the phone calls progressed, the chemistry between us became palpable. Late-night conversations replaced formalities, and genuine curiosity led to discussions that touched upon the essence of our personalities.

Mayank: (seriously) Ishita, do you believe in second chances?

Ishita: (contemplative) Absolutely. Sometimes life gives us opportunities we never expected.

The vulnerability in our voices became a bridge that deepened our connection, a silent understanding growing between us.

Mayank: (tentatively) Ishita, there's something about our conversations that feels different. Am I reading too much into it?

Ishita: (softly) Mayank, maybe what we have is more than just friendship. Maybe it's worth exploring.

The acknowledgment of our feelings opened a new chapter in our connection, one that hold the promise of shared emotions and the potential for something more.

In conclusion, what began as a chance meeting at the bank blossomed into a series of phone calls that transcended the ordinary. Brought together by a shared connection and genuine conversations, we discovered a bond that went beyond the surface. The phone calls, filled with laughter, dreams, and the subtle exploration of emotions, became the foundation for a connection that held the promise of possibilities yet to unfold.

The year unfolded, and our friendship continued to flourish. What started as a routine banking interaction during Dussehra had transformed into a genuine bond that transcended the confines of the bank.

As we navigated the ever-changing landscape of our individual journeys, our connection remained a constant. The bank, initially just a space for financial transactions, had become a backdrop to a story of friendship and celebration. Dussehra, the auspicious beginning, continued to be a reminder of the serendipity that had unfolded on that crisp autumn evening in 2017.

Chapter XII

Old Flames

As I reminisce about the year 2018, memories of my time at the Madhavnagar Katni branch come flooding back. It was a period of transition and growth, both personally and professionally. Little did I know that an unexpected phone call would soon shake up my world and bring back memories of a past long forgotten.

It had been years since I last spoke to Rasika, my ex-girlfriend. Yes, even today writing "Ex-Girlfriend" makes me go back in time with all the memories that I lived and shared with her. Our breakup had been amicable, yet the pain of losing her lingered for a while before gradually fading away as life moved on. I had begun to forget her, or at least I thought I had, until that fateful day when my phone rang unexpectedly, and her name flashed across the screen.

My heart skipped a beat as I answered the call, a flood of emotions rushing through me. "Hello?" I said tentatively, unsure of what to expect.

"Hi, it's me," came Rasika's voice on the other end, her tone hesitant yet familiar.

I was taken aback by her call, unsure of how to respond. "Rasika? It's been… it's been a long time," I replied, my voice betraying a hint of uncertainty.

There was a moment of silence as we both grappled with the weight of our past and the uncertainty of our present. "I know, I know," Rasika finally said, her voice soft yet filled with emotion. "I've been meaning to call you for a while now, but… but I just didn't know how to start."

I could hear the hesitation in her voice, mirroring my own feelings of confusion and apprehension. "It's okay," I reassured her, my heart pounding in my chest. "I'm here now. What's on your mind?"

Rasika took a deep breath before speaking, her words measured yet filled with longing. "I've been thinking a lot lately, about us, about what we had… and I realized that I never truly moved on," she admitted, her voice tinged with regret.

I felt a knot form in my stomach as her words washed over me. Despite the passage of time, the memories of our relationship still held a powerful grip on both of us. "I understand," I said softly, struggling to find the right words. "I've had my moments too, where I've wondered… wondered if things could have been different."

There was a shared sense of vulnerability between us, a mutual acknowledgment of the pain and longing that had brought us back together. "I miss you," Rasika confessed, her voice barely above a whisper.

My heart ached at her words, a bittersweet reminder of the love we had once shared. "I miss you too," I admitted, my voice filled with emotion. "I've tried to move on, to forget... but some part of me always held onto the hope that maybe, just maybe, we'd find our way back to each other."

As we spoke, the years melted away, and it was as if we were transported back to a time when our love was still young and innocent. We laughed, we cried, we reminisced about the moments that had shaped our relationship, both the good and the bad.

But amidst the nostalgia, there was also a sense of uncertainty lingering in the air. We were both different people now, shaped by the passage of time and the experiences that had shaped our lives. Could we truly find our way back to each other, or were we destined to remain nothing more than faded memories of a love long gone?

As the conversation drew to a close, there was a sense of reluctance in both of our voices. "I don't know what the future holds," Rasika said softly, her words echoing my own thoughts. "But I'm glad we had this talk. It feels like... like a weight has been lifted off my shoulders."

I couldn't help but agree. Despite the uncertainty of what lay ahead, there was a sense of closure in our conversation, a newfound clarity that had eluded us for so long. "Me too," I said, my voice filled with gratitude. "Thank you, Rasika, for reaching out. It means more to me than you'll ever know."

And with that, we said our goodbyes, both of us left to ponder the significance of our unexpected reunion. The road ahead may be uncertain, but one thing was for certain - the memories of our love would always hold a special place in both of our hearts, no matter where life may lead us.

And as I closed my eyes and let the tears fall, I knew that no matter what the future held, Rasika's call had brought us one step closer to finding the closure we both so desperately needed.

www.ingramcontent.com/pod-product-compliance
Lightning Source LLC
La Vergne TN
LVHW041151150826
845673LV00001B/133

* 9 7 9 8 8 9 3 6 3 6 2 6 0 *